# Just a Cowboy's Love Song

Flyboys of Sweet Briar Ranch in North Dakota
Book Ten
Jessie Gussman

Published By: Jessie Gussman

# Contents

# Acknowledgments

**Cover art by Julia Gussman**
**Editing by Heather Hayden**
**Narration by Jay Dyess**
**Author Services by CE Author Assistant**

Listen to a FREE professionally performed and produced audiobook version of this title on Youtube. Search for "Say With Jay" to browse all available FREE Dyess/Gussman audiobooks.

# Chapter 1

Jones hurried down the street, casting a quick glance behind him.

Thankfully he'd left his niece, Florence, at home in the duplex they'd just rented in Sweet Water, North Dakota.

Because the cow was gaining on him.

His horns, at least two feet long on each side of his head, were enough to scare anyone, even someone who worked out regularly as he did.

He didn't quite break into a run, but he lengthened his stride. He didn't particularly want to be seen running from a cow.

He managed to take another ten strides or so before he shot another glance over his shoulder.

Somehow, even though the cow didn't look like it was working hard at all, it had managed to gain on him.

He could almost feel the hot breath on the backs of his arms.

Sweat broke out on his brow, and his heart pounded like he'd been jogging for six miles instead of walking for two blocks.

He tucked the takeout that he'd gotten from the diner in town up under his arm.

He had no groceries in the house, and the takeout was all he had to feed his niece. He really didn't think this cow wanted the takeout; he was leaning more toward the idea that the cow wanted *him.*

Still, he hoped both the takeout and himself would manage to make it to the duplex before the cow. What did cows do?

Did they eat people?

Or was he just going to grind him into a messy pulp with his horns?

He'd seen enough bull riding to know horns were dangerous.

Speaking of, something brushed the back of his arm, and he would have forgotten his good intentions and broken into a dead sprint, since his house was only two blocks away, except he noticed a young girl walking toward him.

She didn't seem the slightest bit afraid of this cow in front of her and was actually looking at Jones like there might be something wrong with *him*.

She didn't stop, didn't turn, and... Was she talking to the cow?

"Billy? What are you doing following someone down the sidewalk? You have no manners."

The girl was tall, but she looked to be about the same age as Florence, his niece.

He took a deep breath, and maybe he should have stopped, or maybe he shouldn't have tried to keep one eye on the girl and one eye on the cow.

Whatever it was, he didn't see the crack in the sidewalk and tripped over it.

He went down, dropping the takeout and landing on top of it. A jolt of pain went up through his hip, and his elbow scraped on the cement.

It was embarrassing. He was known as being quite athletic. Despite the fact that he was a musician by trade, he hit the gym regularly and looked like it.

It was a blow to his pride to be looking up at the girl from his inglorious position on the sidewalk.

But fear was more like a dagger to his heart as the cow stopped, standing directly over top of him, his horns looking even bigger from that angle.

"Are you okay?" the girl said, coming over and putting one hand on the cow's forehead, pushing.

The cow, acting all docile now that the girl was a witness to their interactions, backed up so that he was able to lower his head and put his nose directly in front of Jones's nose.

He wasn't sure whether that was an improvement or not. Particularly if this cow was hungry and intended to eat him.

He supposed he would rather the beast start at his head. It would make his demise faster and less painful.

"Billy. Stop being a brat. Back up and let the man up." The girl, her tone soft, still sounded irritated. "This is no way to welcome people to town. You're going to scare them away instead of keeping them around."

"Thanks," he said as the cow backed up even farther, making Jones feel like he could get up, even though he scooted backward a little bit before he did so he didn't have to turn his back on the beast.

"Billy is not usually like this," the girl said, shaking her head.

He wanted to say, "What? Does he typically eat people feetfirst?" But he didn't.

"He doesn't usually chase people down?" he said instead.

"Nah. He loves to be petted, but he doesn't usually target people on the sidewalk."

Jones looked down at his ruined takeout. He had been hoping to be able to get back to his duplex and take it easy for the rest of the day. He supposed that idea was out of the question.

But he didn't want to go back to the diner either. If this cow was attacking innocent people on the sidewalk, he might need to find a different town to settle down in for a while.

"I'm sorry about your food," the girl said, looking at the smashed white Styrofoam boxes on the ground.

He shook his head, bending over and shaking the food out of the boxes before picking the containers up. "It's not your fault. It's mine. I didn't see the crack in the sidewalk."

"I distracted you," the girl said.

He shook his head. It wasn't her fault.

"I'm Jones," he said, putting both boxes in one hand and holding his other out for the girl to shake.

She smiled a little, the way he would imagine Florence would if some strange man offered to shake her hand. Like it made her feel like she was a grown-up. Then she took his hand and shook it with a grip that was surprisingly firm. "I'm Toni."

"Nice to meet you, Toni."

"It's nice to meet you too. I... I guess you're new in town?"

"Is it that obvious?"

"Well, not really, except everyone in town knows Billy. That's the steer."

Not a cow. A steer. He tried to take note of the difference.

"Oh. I guess that was an introduction." He eyed the steer. "I would say it's nice to meet him, but I haven't determined that as of yet."

The girl giggled, and Jones smiled despite himself.

He wasn't really angry at the animal. Getting angry at a cow seemed silly, but he had to say he was annoyed. He wasn't used to being chased down the sidewalk and forced to feel like he needed to run for his life.

The ruined food magnified that feeling.

The girl looked at the sidewalk, and then she lifted her head quickly as though she just thought of something. "My mom has food in the crockpot for tonight. It's really good. And... I know she's going to be working because she said she had a late meeting, but I know she wouldn't mind if you came over and ate some?"

"Oh, I couldn't invite myself like that," Jones said. "Plus, my niece...lives with me." He stumbled over that because he still hadn't gotten used to explaining that his niece was now his. It wasn't that long ago that his sister died in the airplane crash.

"I promise you, Mom always makes a lot, and then we eat the leftovers. But people are always welcome at our table. Mom says that all the time."

Jones shook his head and moved a little. The girl moved with him, and they ended up walking side by side toward his house.

He didn't look back, but he had the feeling the cow, *steer*, was still following him.

He managed not to run.

"I couldn't impose like that."

The girl lifted a shoulder like it didn't matter. "If you change your mind, we live right up here."

"Interesting. I live up here too. I just rented half of the duplex right there."

"You're our new neighbor!" Toni said, her jaw dropping as she looked at him with wide eyes. "I saw there was someone moving in before I left for school today, but I didn't see you. I thought there might be a girl my age."

"I think Florence probably is your age."

"Then you have to come for supper! Whatever time you want. Like I said, Mom will be working so it'll just be me, and I'll wait until you guys show up."

Jones had already declined two or three times, and so he didn't shake his head again. It wouldn't hurt to go over to the neighbors' house and have supper.

Maybe, once the ranch remodel was finished, which shouldn't be long now that he was here to oversee the work, he could invite her and her mom out to eat there, and maybe they'd have animals by then and they'd enjoy looking around the ranch.

He wasn't sure what all the ranch was going to have eventually. His sister had been the one with all the big plans. He'd inherited that along with half of everything she left. The other half went to Florence, and he managed it until she turned eighteen.

The thought of his sister and her plane accident still sent a sharp knife of pain down his ribs, and he pulled his mind away.

It might have been a year, but it hardly felt that long.

Although he was able to think of it now without the sad longing and the deep desire to somehow bring her back that he used to have.

"We have a little table on our porch. You'll see when we get there. I'll just bring everything out and set it on that. If you want to come out and eat with me, you can. And if you don't, don't feel like you have to. The weather is nice enough that I'll be happy eating outside, so you'll be doing me a favor."

Jones looked down at the girl. He knew, in the year since his sister had died, that Florence was lonely. She'd often mentioned that she'd like to have a little brother or sister.

Maybe this girl was lonely too.

"All right. I'll watch for you to go out on your porch, and I'll come over."

He should get out and meet the neighbors anyway. This would be a good way to do that. Even if he didn't meet the mom. Or the dad. Although she hadn't mentioned a dad.

He didn't ask though; that could be a sensitive subject. After all, if someone asked Florence where her parents were for the first six months after her mother's death, she would have started to cry.

Now, he thought that she was slowly healing as he was. And he didn't think she would break down. But...it would definitely make her sad.

So, he looked around for something neutral to talk about, and out of the corner of his eye, he saw the steer was still following them.

"Who owns that steer anyway?" he asked, refraining from saying that they needed to get their animal and make sure he was penned up.

"The town. No one really knows who exactly owns him, and we all kind of take care of him. He's like our own town mascot. We even use him in the petting zoo when we have a festival in town. The kids love him."

"I see." Well, there went that idea. Apparently he was going to be dealing with the steer every time he set foot out of his house since he seemed to be a cow magnet.

"Does he normally chase people down and eat them?" he asked, trying to put a teasing tone in his voice but not entirely sure he succeeded.

"No. You're the first." Toni must have caught the teasing note, because her eyes twinkled when she looked up at him.

He smiled down at her and thought again that she would make a perfect playmate for Florence. Maybe it was a good thing he had accepted her dinner invitation.

He was pretty sure Florence wouldn't turn it down either, and she would possibly have someone to hang out with on her first day of school. There were only a couple of weeks left before summer break, but he was going to enroll her anyway. She had such up-heaval in her young life so far, he wanted to give her a sense of normalcy if he could.

They reached the steps of the duplex, his side on the right, Toni's on the left. He saw the table she meant. Some kind of privacy shield hung above the railing that separated the two sides.

He didn't think his new neighbors were going to be annoying, but if they were, that privacy shield would probably come in handy.

"It will be about thirty minutes until I have the food ready, but you can come out whenever you want to."

"Thanks." They separated, and he walked into his house, humming under his breath.

That was new. Since his sister's death, the idea of singing had been depressing. He definitely didn't hum out of happiness. Except, now he was. Interesting.

# Chapter 2

Mallie Woods pressed her lips together and pushed her head-phones closer to her ears.

She had been taking notes for the entire meeting, after doing an insane amount of work for the previous three weeks to get ready for it. Her boss, Samson Strong, was very demanding and expected her to be Superwoman.

It definitely made her raise the level of her game, but it also exhausted her.

She couldn't wait to get this meeting over, except, from the way things were going, her workload, instead of decreasing, was going to increase. Substantially.

She hadn't had a weekend off in three weeks. And Toni would be getting out of school soon. She wanted to be able to spend time with her daughter, not be working evenings and weekends trying to keep up to Samson's demands.

"That's a great idea, Danielle," Samson said. "I love your go-get-'em attitude, and while it's a little risky, I like risk." His voice lowered a little, like he was giving her a personal compliment. And, to Samson, that probably *was* a personal compliment.

Danielle beamed over the screen.

Samson gave a sexy-looking smile. The man was handsome, even if he was a jerk, and then his eyes shifted.

"Mallie, did you get that? Make sure you put down everything Danielle suggested in bullet points for the follow-up email. I don't want to miss any of it. I want the rest of the team to know."

"Yes, sir," she murmured as she shifted slightly, looking at the second screen on her desk and typing out the last few things Danielle had said.

Dark had fallen a long time ago. She'd only seen her daughter Toni for just a couple of minutes after school before she had to run into the meeting. So far, it had lasted three hours.

"Actually, while I'm thinking about that, that will be your last duty."

At first, Samson's words didn't register as she typed as fast as she could to get Danielle's words down. Then she realized Samson was talking to her. Her head jerked up, and she narrowed her eyes at the screen.

"Me?" she asked, unsure of what exactly he meant by last duty.

"Yes. The technology for AI is coming along quite well, and I've actually been implementing it alongside of the work that I give you. I've gotten to the point where the AI VA that I have is actually more efficient and cheaper," he chuckled, "than you are."

Mallie's stomach sank. What exactly was he saying? It sounded like...he was letting her go.

Her mouth felt dry, like someone had wiped it out with a dry paper towel. She wasn't sure what to say. So she just stared at the screen, knowing her jaw hung open but unable to summon up the brainpower to close it.

"I'd give you severance pay, but I used the money I had allotted for it to fully purchase the AI VA. I'm sure with your skills, you won't have trouble finding another job."

She sat staring at her computer screen, unable to do anything but blink.

After more than five years of complete, almost slave-like devotion to this man, working weekends and evenings, whatever he needed to get the job done, he was going to dump her just like that?

"All right. I still expect that report to be emailed to me before you quit for the week. I'll have the AI assistant change all of my passwords and remove your access to the company completely." Samson looked at his watch, big and expensive. "In fact, we're ending right on time. I have the severance scheduled for eight o'clock." He grinned at the computer screen, looking very satisfied with himself. "That's one of the best things about AI. They don't care what time of day it is. It doesn't tell me that it has to go feed its family. It doesn't complain about evenings, weekends, or holidays. I couldn't be more pleased."

He waved, the satisfied smirk never leaving his face.

Mallie wasn't typically a violent person, and she only thought for about five seconds of the satisfaction she would feel as she grabbed his nose and twisted it as hard as she could.

"Toodles," Danielle said.

The two faces on the screen went dark.

Mallie sat in shock.

She depended on the job to feed her daughter. To pay the rent. She had some money saved. A very small amount of money, but some nonetheless. She'd had to pay for Toni's braces out of pocket since she had no dental insurance, and the co-pay from their ER visit when she'd fallen and sprained her ankle had finished draining her savings.

She tried not to allow herself to panic. Tried to think that there was a purpose in this. God had a plan.

*Lord? I know I'm supposed to trust You, but I'm scared. I don't have very much money and no one else I can depend on except for myself and for You, and now I don't have a job. You know how hard I worked at this job, and...yeah, maybe I was depending on my job more than I was depending on You.*

Funny how some kind of emergency in her life could make a person reevaluate and see things they hadn't been able to see when life had been humming along with everything falling into line the way it was supposed to.

But now that her job had been taken from her, she could see how she had been leaning on that instead of on the Lord.

*Sorry, Lord. I guess I needed this wake-up call, but even knowing that I needed it and actually getting it, it's still scary.*

The idea that she wouldn't be able to pay her rent. That her daughter would starve, that they would be out on the streets, that she would have to rely on the generosity and charity of her neighbors in order to eat, scared her.

She didn't want to be beholden to anyone. She'd been brought up to work hard and to earn her own way.

*Isn't that pride?*

She knew pride was something the Lord hated. **God resisted the proud, but giveth grace to the humble.** The verse went through her head, and she contemplated the idea that her aversion to taking charity was because of pride.

She wanted to think it was because she wanted to work and be a contributing member of society, not someone who just took and never gave back.

That wasn't pride, was it?

She laughed at herself. She just got fired from her job, had no clue what she was going to do, and she was worried about being too proud.

Sometimes she found the strangest things to get all upset about.

Staying in her seat for another moment, she pulled in a deep, slow breath, holding it until she counted to eight, trying to focus her mind on the idea that God would take care of her, and she did not have to worry.

She reached a slow eight count and then began to blow the breath out, a steady, easy exhale, blowing through her lips and imagining all of her stress and problems blowing out with it.

She could do this. God was not surprised at how her life turned out today. He had known all along this was going to happen. And

He knew exactly what He was going to do for her in the future. She didn't have to stress.

She might have to work, it might be uncomfortable, and she might have to think outside the box, doing things she might not have thought she ever would, but a lot of times what looked like the worst thing in a person's life could turn out to be the best thing, and she was determined, if she had anything to do with it, that's exactly what this would be.

Even if she couldn't see how that could possibly happen.

Pushing up from her desk, she stood, stretching. She switched her computer off, decided she'd send the follow-up email before bed, and strode to the door of her closet, which was also her office.

Her ex had been a terrible husband and even worse father, and thankfully she only had one daughter. So the two-bedroom duplex was big enough for her daughter to have one room and her to have the other.

She would love for her office to have a window, but she was grateful that at least she had an office.

Moving slowly down the stairs, knowing that she would have to tell Toni that she would be looking for work, she followed her nose to the kitchen.

There were less leftovers than what she thought there should be, and she wondered if Toni had had her friends over to eat.

At twelve years old, Toni was old enough to take care of herself, and she had never given Mallie any trouble at all.

Mallie had tried to make sure that Toni knew her friends were always welcome at their house. Her philosophy had been that if her daughter knew her friends were welcome here, she wouldn't feel like they needed to sneak out in order to meet.

She hadn't gotten to the teenage stage yet, but so far so good.

It was a warm late May evening, and she figured Toni might be sitting on the porch since she didn't see her in the kitchen nor the living room.

Getting a plate of food from the leftovers, she grabbed a glass of water from the faucet and then carried her plate and silverware in one hand and her cup in the other as she pushed open the door.

She heard singing and smiled as she recognized an old hymn.

The man's voice sounded strangely familiar, although she was fairly certain she hadn't heard it before.

She had seen when she had hugged her daughter goodbye that morning before school that it looked like they were getting neighbors on the other side of the duplex. As she listened to the hymn being sung, she smiled that God would have provided Christian fellowship just when she needed it most, and right next door to her.

It was dark. Probably because of the cloud cover which helped the heat stay trapped in the atmosphere and allowed the night air to be warmer than it normally might have been. It also made seeing anything quite hard.

Looking over, she couldn't tell where her neighbors were sitting, and she didn't want to turn her porch light on and interrupt the sweet atmosphere that seemed to have enveloped their porches.

She could hear her daughter humming along and loved that she seemed to enjoy just sitting on the porch, singing, or in her case humming.

She wasn't sure what she had done to deserve such a great daughter. She wasn't going to look that gift horse in the mouth but said a silent prayer of thanks, once again, to the Lord for the wonderful blessing her daughter had become.

Sitting down, she ate as her neighbor strummed his guitar and continued to sing, moving from one hymn into another.

She was familiar with every hymn he sang and was impressed that he knew all the verses.

A lot of people could quote some words to the first line and probably knew the chorus very well, but this man sang all the words to all the verses.

She couldn't see if his wife was out with him. If she was, she wasn't singing along.

As she finished up her meal, swallowing the last bit of her water and setting everything aside, she pushed gently on the swing. Rocking just a little.

She listened as her neighbor finished his current hymn, plucked a note on his guitar, then started a new one a cappella.

*My Jesus, I love thee, I know thou art mine;*

As soon as she heard it, she recognized it and started singing harmony.

*for thee all the follies of sin I resign;*
*my gracious Redeemer, my Savior art thou;*
*if ever I loved thee, my Jesus, 'tis now.*

He had to have noticed her singing, but he didn't say anything and continued on with the second verse while she joined him. Toni, who probably didn't know the words, hummed along.

*I love thee because thou hast first loved me*
*and purchased my pardon on Calvary's tree;*
*I love thee for wearing the thorns on thy brow;*
*if ever I loved thee, my Jesus, 'tis now.*

This was one of her favorite hymns, and she didn't have any trouble remembering the words. They came to her mind naturally as she closed her eyes and forgot about the problems of the day and just focused on the timeless message of the sweet, old hymn.

*I'll love thee in life, I will love thee in death,*
*and praise thee as long as thou lendest me breath,*
*and say when the deathdew lies cold on my brow:*
*If ever I loved thee, my Jesus, 'tis now.*

*In mansions of glory and endless delight,*
*I'll ever adore thee in heaven so bright;*
*I'll sing with the glittering crown on my brow:*
*If ever I loved thee, my Jesus, 'tis now.*

The last strands had barely faded off into the distance when a girl's voice, sounding like she was about the age of Toni, said, "Uncle Jones, would you do 'Meet Me There,' please?"

There was a grunt of assent as the guitar started strumming softly again.

Mallie, relaxed and at peace from the hymn, the harmonies and the beautiful words of comfort they'd just sung, was somewhat startled when her phone started to buzz in her pocket.

Pulling it out, she saw that it was one of her few friends at the company where she had worked up until just an hour or so ago.

Grabbing her plate and cup, she slipped back inside without interrupting the impromptu sing-along that was going on around her, since both Toni and the girl had joined "Uncle Jones," whoever that was, and were singing.

Her friend had called to offer her condolences and to say that she had no idea she was going to be fired.

Mallie understood, she would feel bad if it had been her friend instead of her, and she would have called to say the same thing.

They chatted for a few minutes, with Mallie not being able to answer any questions—she didn't know what she was going to do, where she was going to go, what job she was going to try to get, and they hung up shortly after. While she was inside, she got her last email for Samson ready to go in and hit send.

She sat at her desk, thinking, when Toni came up and knocked softly on her bedroom door.

"Come on in," she said, shutting her computer down and standing up.

She had a desk downstairs that she used when Toni was in school. She preferred that because there were windows in the living room. But especially when she had meetings, she had to use the closet.

"Hey, Mom. Why did you leave?"

"I had a phone call." She paused. Did she really want to get into the fact that she had gotten fired tonight?

Tomorrow was Friday, and Toni had to go to school. She didn't want her to worry, and Toni, having grown up most of her life without a father, already had a tendency to be anxious about her mother.

She had not shielded her daughter from every little thing that had gone on in her life, believing that kids responded better if they felt like they were part of the family rather than shut out of all of the issues and problems.

For her anyway, she wanted to feel like a part of the solution rather than have things hidden from her.

But she made a spur-of-the-moment decision to wait until tomorrow afternoon to mention her firing, waiting until after Toni got home from school so she would have the entire weekend to adjust to the information.

"Are you still working?" Toni asked, biting down on her lip.

"I just finished." She didn't mention that it would be the last time she worked late. At least for Samson Strong.

"Are you going to have a lot of work to do this weekend?" Toni asked.

"No." That was the easy answer. Then, before Toni could question her further, she said, "Did you meet the neighbors? Or did you just go out and they were singing?"

"I rescued him from Billy."

"The town steer?"

Toni grinned, nodding her head. "Yeah. For some reason, Billy was following him down the street. He had takeout from the diner, which he was taking home for his niece. I invited them, and we had supper together."

"That's why there weren't a lot of leftovers."

"Yeah, I knew you wouldn't mind if I offered to share because the takeout he was carrying got smashed when he tripped over the sidewalk and fell on top of it." She paused. "I don't know why Billy was following him."

Mallie couldn't answer that question either. That steer was an odd one. A lot of residents claimed it was a matchmaking steer, and they gave really good evidence to back up their claims. But Mallie still wasn't sure she believed them.

After all, it certainly hadn't matched her up with anyone. Not that she had wanted to be. Toni had begged and begged for her to get married again, but... Her first marriage had been such a disaster. She didn't want to go through that all again, no matter how much easier having someone to share her life with might make it.

There was always give-and-take in a relationship, and she felt like she'd already been in a relationship that was so much more give than take, at least on her end. She didn't want to do that again. She had a tendency to tell herself that she was terrible at picking men, and she should just cut her losses and get out of the game.

"I'm not sure why Billy does what he does. He seems to turn up everywhere though. So I guess it's not too surprising that he attached himself to someone who is new in town. Maybe he was going to give him a tour or something."

"Mom. Really?"

Mallie shrugged. To her that sounded just as reasonable as the people who insisted he was some kind of matchmaker.

But she didn't say that to Toni. She didn't want to be as cynical as she felt. In fact, she wanted to be something completely different. A kind, considerate, loving person, who always thought the best of everyone.

And every cow, too, she supposed.

"Anyway, he apparently has a niece who lives with him, and she's my age. He was going to take her to school tomorrow and enroll her, but since it's Friday and they...have a ranch or something somewhere that's getting work or something..." Toni's voice trailed off like she had heard him explain it, but she hadn't picked up on everything. "Anyway, he's going to take her Monday and enroll her in school even though there are only two weeks left. And she seems really nice, and I'm going to have a friend living right beside me. At least until they move to their ranch."

For some reason, the idea that neighbors who sang hymns on their porch in the dark would not be around for very long made Mallie sad. Living in a duplex, she wasn't guaranteed what kind of neighbor she got, and bad ones could really make her life miserable. She'd lived through a few of those, although thankfully they hadn't stayed long.

Still, she appreciated having good ones for whatever time they stayed.

"And how was school today? How do you think you did on your math test? And did you get your English essay back?"

Toni started talking about school, and the test she took, and the things that were happening for the end of the year, and they didn't talk any more about their neighbors, although Mallie couldn't help but wonder why the man was living with his niece and where his wife was.

At least that gave her brain something to think about, something more than the fact that she lost her job and had no idea what she was going to do, other than start a major job search in the morning.

# Chapter 3

"**G**ood morning," Mallie said as Toni stumbled into the kitchen the next day. Normally Toni woke up smiling and bright, but currently she looked bleary and like she hadn't slept very well.

"Are you okay?" Mallie asked, moving from the stove where she had just poured eggs into a skillet. She didn't always make breakfast. Sometimes she was already working at this time in the morning and just took a few minutes to give her daughter a hug and tell her to have a good day at school.

But since she didn't have a job anymore, there was no reason for her not to be cooking a healthy breakfast for her.

"Yeah. I'm fine," Toni said, her voice not matching the message of her words.

But Toni was notorious for not wanting to miss any school. Anytime she was sick, Mallie had to make her stay home, because she wouldn't choose to do so herself.

Mallie walked over, putting her hand on Toni's forehead. "You don't have a fever," she murmured. "Did you have trouble sleeping?"

Toni shook her head, then she walked to the cupboard and got two plates.

Mallie narrowed her eyes at her before walking back to the stove.

Something was up, but she wasn't sure what it was.

As for herself, she did have a little bit of trouble falling asleep but had ended up just praying. Asking the Lord to help her not worry about the future, knowing it was in God's hands. Knowing that this was one of the times where she had to live her faith and live what she said she believed. If she thought God was in control of the future, and God cared for her and loved her, then she wasn't going to worry about whether or not she got a job. Of course, she was human too, and a sense of failure, a sense of sadness and loss, a sense of unfairness, the desire to be angry and bitter, were all things she had been fighting.

Still, her job was to take care of her daughter, who looked terrible.

"Is there something you want to talk to me about?" she asked as Toni listlessly put silverware next to the plates and grabbed cups from the cupboard.

Toni's brows went down, as though she were confused and wondering what in the world her mom was talking about.

That made Mallie think that maybe she wasn't hiding anything. She never had trouble with that in the past, and it was a relief to think that it wasn't a problem yet.

She always tried to be available to talk to Toni, always tried to be sure Toni knew she could talk to her about anything.

Still, there was something wrong.

Turning back the stove, she flipped the eggs then peeled two pieces of cheese off and put them over top.

Snapping the burner off, she grabbed the skillet and carried it the short distance to the table, putting half of the eggs on her plate and half on Toni's.

She set the skillet back on a cold burner and grabbed the salsa. She set it down on the table and sat down in her seat.

The smell of freshly cooked eggs made her stomach growl. She wouldn't mind not ever working again and being able to cook breakfast every morning.

She supposed it would get old after a while, but after having to work for so many years and grabbing cold cereal or something easy, it was nice to have the time to sit at the table and actually be able to look at her child.

Who still didn't look well. She seemed white and even a little pasty.

Bowing her head, Mallie said a short prayer, adding in her heart a plea to the Lord to help her job search be fruitful today so she didn't go very long without employment.

Toni whispered an amen, and they picked up their silverware, eating in silence for a bit.

Mallie was deep in thought, thinking about where she was going to start her job search, when Toni's fork clattered to the table. Mallie looked up in time to see Toni's eyes get big before she shot up and ran to the garbage can. She made it just in time.

Mallie got up and followed her more slowly, putting an arm around her and pulling her hair back away from her face as her daughter threw up in the can.

It made her own stomach turn to hear the sounds and to smell the warm, tangy scent of puke.

She didn't bother to look at the chewed-up eggs and salsa in the garbage can.

Her daughter finally heaved a couple of times and nothing came up, while Mallie took her hair in one hand and slipped her arm around her, pulling her back toward the table.

"Sit down. I'll get you a little water."

Toni nodded but didn't say anything.

"I think I feel better now," Toni whispered a few moments later after she'd taken a couple of sips of water and sat with her hand holding her head.

"You need to stay home from school today," Mallie said firmly, knowing Toni was going to protest.

"But I feel better!" she said, looking up at her mom with pleading in her eyes.

Mallie steeled her heart. She couldn't let her daughter throw up in the morning and go to school ten minutes later. That wasn't responsible.

"If you feel better, you can go in at lunchtime."

Toni's lips pressed together. "I'd rather not go in at all then."

"All right. If you feel like going back up to lie down, you can, but I think it would be a good idea if you don't eat anything for a couple of hours and let your stomach settle."

Toni nodded, probably unsurprised, because the few times that she'd puked before in her life, that had always been Mallie's solution. She didn't know whether that actually worked or not, but at least it kept the puke cleanup to a minimum.

Her daughter walked slowly out of the room, after Mallie had asked her if there was anything she could do and Toni had shaken her head and said, "Unless you're going to let me go to school."

Mallie just shook her head and smiled.

It was funny to her that most people had problems with getting their kids to want to go to school, and she had a child that did not want to miss.

Regardless, her job search might be a little bit more difficult considering that Toni would be around during the day. She had to be careful that Toni didn't overhear her talking on the phone.

Maybe she should have told Toni about losing her job. But she had been so concerned about what might have been wrong with Toni that she hadn't considered it.

Later. Maybe at lunch. Or supper.

With that, she cleaned the table off, putting the dishes in the sink and figuring she would take care of them later, eager to get a plan in place for her life. She didn't like being unemployed, didn't like not knowing what the future held. Although, as she'd learned yesterday, what she thought the future was going to be might not pan out. But it made her feel more secure to think that she had some control over things and some idea of what was going to happen.

Three hours later, Mallie laid her head down on the table in the dining room. Most companies went through some kind of online application process. She'd filled out more than her share, dusting off her resume and updating it, and texting a few people to make sure it was okay to use them as references.

Actually getting something done had made her feel great, like she was accomplishing something and doing something productive.

But as she looked at all of the other updated, happy profiles of the other professionals on the work employment website she was on, she felt like she would never measure up.

Many of them were not work-from-home positions, and the few that she found still made moving necessary.

She didn't want to have to move. She didn't want to have to have her daughter change schools. She didn't want to have to put down roots somewhere else, build friendships, and reestablish a sense of community. She definitely didn't want to have to move to the city, but that seemed to be where all the opportunities were, of course.

Taking a breath, letting it out slowly, she allowed a few tears to roll down her face.

Lifting her head, she looked out the window at the scene which was mostly of the house beside her, but the sun and some blue sky was visible if she craned her head, and she could see Billy standing on the sidewalk.

That made her smile, but it also made her eyes fill with more tears.

Sweet Water was a special place. She didn't want to have to leave. She loved it here. Loved the people, loved the way the town rallied around people, loved everything about it.

"Mom?"

Mallie jerked her head around, swiping at the tears on her cheeks but knowing that she wasn't going to be able to hide them from her daughter.

"Mom? What's wrong?" Toni's voice was filled with concern as she hurried across the room to put her arms around her mom. "Did Mr. Samson yell at you again?"

Toni had no idea how many times Samson had made her cry. Actually, Samson had no idea how many times Samson had made her cry. She couldn't cry while he was telling her what she had done wrong and berating her for it, which was especially hurtful when he did it in front of colleagues on video chats.

But she'd always been able to hold her tears back until she turned her camera off and cried in private. Usually Toni was at school.

But apparently, the times Toni had caught her had marked her more than Mallie thought.

"No. Samson didn't berate me about anything. But maybe you had better sit down. I have something I need to tell you."

"Are you sick?" Toni asked, probably coming up with the worst-case scenario she could think of. That made Mallie smile. That her daughter would care about her and her being sick was the worst thing she could think of happening.

"No. But yesterday... Samson told me that he no longer needed me. I've been...job searching all morning."

"Why are you crying? Did someone tell you they wouldn't hire you?"

"No. No one said that. And I think I have a couple of pretty good prospects. I just..." Could she confess her fear to Toni? She'd always tried to be as upright and honest as she could, but she didn't want to upset Toni's world.

But maybe it would be best if she gave her a little bit of warning. She would rather have an idea of what she could pray for than be blindsided with news.

"A lot of the jobs I have applied for would mean that we would have to move out of Sweet Water."

"Move?" Toni asked, her eyes growing big and a bit of anger crossing her face. Maybe a little belligerence. Toni didn't want to move any more than Mallie did.

"I know. I'm going to try as hard as I can to find a job where we don't have to, but... I guess I was just a little frustrated and discouraged."

"Why didn't you tell me this morning?" Toni asked, irritation in her tone.

"You were sick. I didn't want to make it worse."

"I felt better as soon as I threw up. And I've been resting all morning. I... I thought I might want to go to school, but I think I'd rather not."

Mallie's heart sank. Her news had made Toni sad. She'd known it would, she'd just been hoping... She didn't know. Sometimes it was hard to be a mom and try to figure out what her daughter needed to know and what she shouldn't be told. Maybe she should have just kept her news to herself. All of it. But then, how would she explain the crying?

"I know this is scary. It's scary for me too. And it's not really something I wanted to have to deal with. I knew last night before I went to bed, and I was talking to God about it a little bit. I know I've said all my life about how I trust God, and how I know He loves me, and how I know He cares for me, and then something like this happens, and all of a sudden, I get scared and upset and angry and wonder what's going to happen. That's not really living what I believe, is it?"

Toni shook her head slowly.

"Maybe you feel the same way," she said, and Toni nodded. "But that's not the way we should feel if we trust the Lord to do His very best for us, right?"

Toni shook her head again.

"So, last night, I had to say, I trust you, Lord. Whatever You're going to do, wherever You're going to take us, whatever job I'm going to get, whatever You put in my path, I will open the door—whatever open door You give me, I will walk through it."

She looked at her daughter, thinking that Toni seemed to understand.

"I guess it's times like these where we're scared, and only want to cling to earthly things to make us feel better, that we have to step up by faith and trust that God has something perfect planned for us."

Toni nodded, and Mallie put her arm around her. Toni leaned closer, putting her head on Mallie's shoulder and allowing Mallie to pull her tight.

"I was thinking a little bit about Abraham and how he took Isaac up as a sacrifice. You know the story."

"Yeah." Toni's response was mumbled as she said it against Mallie's chest.

"Of course God delivered him, but Abraham had to go up the mountain first. He had to build an altar. He had to tie Isaac up and put him on it and be ready to deliver the killing blow before God stopped him and saved Isaac. God just wanted to see how much Abraham was willing to give up. He didn't require Abraham to give up everything, He just wanted to see how much he would. You know?"

Toni shook her head yes.

Mallie knew she was a little bit young to understand, but even if she didn't get it now, the lessons that she was being taught might solidify later in her life. So Mallie kept talking.

"Sometimes God takes everything away, just to see what we're depending on, and a lot of times, at least for me anyway, I'm surprised to see that I've been depending on myself, or on my job, or on something else, for my security. And I haven't been depending on God. Now, just because we depend on God doesn't mean that all of our problems magically disappear. Even though God delivered the Israelites from the Egyptians, the Israelites still had to do the work of packing up and leaving. They had to have the faith to walk through the Red Sea, with the walls of water on either side. I don't know about you, but that would have been a little bit scary for me."

"That it would crash down around you?"

"Yeah. You had to trust God to hold the walls of water back."

"But God doesn't do miracles today."

"Says who?" Mallie asked, knowing that she couldn't point to any specific miracle in her own life, but she could point to God's provision and protection.

"Not like He used to."

"Maybe not, but He still loves us and He still cares for us and He still wants us to trust Him. And if I'm going to say that I trust Him, it's kind of pointless unless I back that up with works. That's what James means when he said faith without works is dead. I can say I have faith if I want to, but if I refuse to go where God leads me, then I don't really have a living faith."

Toni nodded, and Mallie was pretty sure she understood.

"Did you want to say anything?" she finally said, when Toni just lay against her shoulder, allowing her to stroke her arm and pull her close, like she was much younger than her almost thirteen years.

"No. I know you're right. And I still don't want to leave, I don't want to move anywhere, I don't want to leave my friends. But I understand what you're saying. Sometimes God requires sacrifice. And He wants to know if I'm willing to give it. I... I don't want to, but... I do know that God knows best." She paused. "Unless He's going to take you away. And then I don't want to make that sacrifice."

Toni's words made Mallie's heart smile. She knew they were sincere and that Toni really did want to follow the Lord, even though she was doing it in her little girl way.

"We don't know what the future holds, but most likely God is not going to ask you to make that kind of sacrifice. I guess I could say the same thing: I don't want God to take you from me, and I really don't think He's going to do that. If He does...we'll cross that bridge when we come to it. Because that just means that we need to lean harder on Him and get stronger."

Toni sighed.

"Sometimes I feel like if I trust God, and I say that I'll give Him whatever He wants, I feel like He's going to take everything," Toni whispered softly.

Mallie could relate. She had felt the same way at times over the years. "Can't we say, if He does, it's for our good? Don't we know for sure that everything He does is for our good? Can we be happy with nothing except for God?"

"I don't want to try."

"I don't think He's going to make you, but I do think He wants the attitude that we're willing as long as He goes with us." She sighed. "But that's a really hard attitude for anyone to have, especially so at your age. But I guess just like we can't love perfectly, we can't have perfect faith, and we can't have perfect trust either. We're just not perfect. But sometimes that soothes my soul when I'm scared and unsure. I just know that God's going to work it out for my good. Everything that happens is working for me, not against me, because God is on my side."

Toni didn't say anything more, and Mallie held her, she didn't know how much longer, but eventually Toni got up and said, "I'll cook lunch."

"Guess what? I don't have to work, so I can come help you," Mallie said, giving her a smile and being rewarded with a smile in return.

Toni always enjoyed doing things with her, and that was one of the blessings of being fired from her job. She could spend as much time in the kitchen with Toni as she wanted to today. And if Toni felt better, maybe they could even go to the park or take a walk somewhere.

With that thought, the thought that she would spend the afternoon with her daughter, Mallie got up and, with her arm around Toni, they walked to the kitchen.

# Chapter 4

Jones put his phone back in his pocket and looked at his niece. She looked as bored as a teenager could possibly look.

"Hey, Flo, what do you think?" Jones asked, trying to infuse some excitement into his own voice.

It was hard to imagine this ranch, and all the dreams that his sister had had for it, coming to fruition without her.

But it was just one more thing he had to get used to. His whole life had been hard to imagine without her. Raising her daughter was hard to imagine without her.

"It's okay, I guess," Flo said, shrugging her shoulders.

"Come on. You know I'm not going to fall for that. What's up?" He had been terrible at being compassionate and concerned. Or maybe just terrible at trying to talk about things. But since he was both mom and dad, he needed Flo to at least tell him what was wrong.

"I liked what we were doing last night. That's the kind of thing we used to do with Mom. And... I don't know... I know we didn't even know those people, not really, but it felt like a family."

He nodded, pressing his lips together and shoving his hands in his front pockets as workmen hurried all around them. There was a crew putting the tile down on the kitchen floor, another crew working on installing more tile upstairs in the bathroom, and yet another crew working on installing the heating and air-conditioning system.

But Flo's words pulled Jones's mind from the crews all around them, and the words that he just had with the foreman overseeing everything, and settled it firmly back on last night.

He'd felt the same way. It felt right and good, singing together in the darkness. He had sung hundreds of times in the exact same way with his sister. They'd written songs together that way. They'd grown up singing like that.

Then last night, it had felt casual and not the slightest bit awkward.

Flo was a good singer in her own right, and the girl that they met, Toni, blended beautifully with her.

And the woman. He hadn't gotten a good look at her, but he figured she would be around his sister's age, since she had a child who seemed to be about the same age as Flo. But it had been dark, and she had left before he'd been able to even talk to her.

Toni had said something about her mom working and having a meeting last night. He'd been surprised to see her at all.

Still, just because they sang well together didn't mean that there would be any other kind of relationship beyond short-term neighbors. He'd rented the duplex for a month, intending to not even use it that long, since he and Flo were sleeping on air mattresses in their respective rooms and living out of suitcases.

He hadn't wanted to move everything into the duplex, just to move it all to the ranch. Of course, the ranch would be furnished with entirely new furniture, and they were just moving personal items, such as clothes and toiletries, into their new home. There were a few little knickknacks and some kitchen items, but almost everything would be new.

"Can we stay in town?" Flo asked, looking up at him with pleading in her eyes. It was hard for him to pull the word "no" out of his chest. He wanted to be able to give her what she asked for, especially because she hardly asked for anything, ever. Since her mom had died, she hadn't exactly retreated into a shell, but she'd been quiet, contemplative, and the times that she smiled, and especially the times that she laughed, were treasured by him.

But he shook his head. "It's fun to sing in the dark, but we can't build this ranch and not live on it."

He said that without adding only when he wasn't on tour. He hoped, anyway.

After all, his name hadn't been the one in bright lights. His sister had always sung lead, and he had sung backup harmony behind her. He'd been fine with his role in the back, and she'd always loved the spotlight. It was an arrangement that suited both of them.

He wasn't sure putting himself out front and center was a recipe for continued success. Especially since it had been a year since he'd been onstage, since his sister's plane crash.

But he had wanted to do what was best for Florence. And he felt that taking a break, having the two of them together, would be the best thing. It had also taken that long to get everything wrapped up back in Tennessee.

It hadn't been his dream to live in North Dakota. Annika wanted to be out West. Jones had been lukewarm about it, but Annika already had the property and already had the plans drawn up and the money allotted. He almost felt like he was doing it for his sister's memory just as much as for Florence.

As for him... He hadn't been too excited about it, until he actually arrived in North Dakota. The wide-open sky, the constant breeze, and the down-home friendliness of the people were likely to win him over. Regardless of how many steers chased him down the sidewalk.

Singing in the dark on the front porch had probably done more to warm him to North Dakota than any single other thing.

Florence wandered away, casually looking out the living room's floor-to-ceiling windows, with her hands behind her back, like she was inspecting it rather than enjoying it.

He studied her for a bit until his phone buzzed in his pocket.

Pulling it out, he swiped. "Hello?"

"Jones. Did I catch you at a good time?" It was his agent, Sebastian.

"Sure. I'm out at the ranch, taking a gander."

"How's it coming?"

"Coming along good. They've got three different crews out here working, and the fourth is supposed to arrive tomorrow. It'll be done by the end of the month. Probably a lot sooner." The foreman had just told him that if all went well, it could be less than two weeks. That made him happy, because the air mattress hurt his back. Except, he supposed he was a little bit like Flo and hoped to meet his neighbors on the porch this evening.

"That's good. You guys gonna start working on some new material?"

Sebastian had wanted Flo to take Annika's place. Flo had the voice for it, although she didn't have Annika's attention-loving personality. She was a lot quieter, content as Jones was to stand in the background, which wasn't necessarily a bad thing. It just didn't always make for good entertainment. However, Flo was young, she could grow into it.

"We've already talked about it. Florence is a little young to be going on tour anyway. If we do anything, it's going to be low-key."

"That's fine. But then you need to be out there, writing, recording, and touring."

"I know. People's attention spans are short, and you don't want them to forget us."

"Exactly. Plus, people will love that comeback story. Annika's brother taking over her career after standing in the background all this time. Or Annika's daughter Florence taking the baton from her mother, while Uncle Jones looks on. What a great, heartwarming story."

"I know." He couldn't argue that it wasn't great PR. And he figured it would probably work too. He was just as comfortable singing with Florence as he was with Annika. Actually, in his opinion, Florence did a better job on some of Annika's songs than Annika did.

He certainly would keep that opinion to himself.

He wasn't trying to make Florence feel worse, and it wasn't in her nature to try to outshine her mom. She had been content to stand in her mother's shadow and look on with pride.

"All right, I'll call you in a couple weeks, see how you're settled in, and hopefully you have some new material for me soon."

"Yeah. You do that."

"You want me to keep an eye out for nannies?" Sebastian asked, in what sounded like a change of subject but really wasn't. They both knew that once things geared up again, Jones would be on the move a lot, and it would be difficult to take Florence everywhere with him. They had talked about finding someone to watch her a couple of times over the past year, but Jones hadn't moved on the idea. Between him and Annika, they tag-teamed as parents.

Florence's father had died in an automobile accident before Florence was even born. He was a nonissue, but Jones and Annika had done their best to make sure that Florence didn't feel the lack.

"You might as well." Jones sighed, knowing the inevitable was coming. He didn't want to get sucked back into work and not have things in place to make Florence's life easier and better. He could take her with him over the summer, but once she was going to school regularly, he didn't want to disrupt her schedule. And he didn't want to leave her home alone, without a familiar and trusted adult chaperone

"I can pick four or five candidates and fly them out to meet you."

"Yeah. Thanks." He appreciated the fact that Sebastian knew that he would want to personally interview the candidates and also have them meet Florence. They had to be willing to move to North Dakota too, so there was that.

They talked about a couple more things, some business deals and ideas, before Sebastian had to take another call and they hung up.

Florence was back, staring out the window, looking at the wide expanse of North Dakota sky. There were no houses in view, and the barn was on the opposite side, so nothing blocked the scenery all the way to the horizon where wild North Dakota ground met wild North Dakota sky.

Jones walked over and stood beside Florence, looking at it with her.

"It's just flat. Just sky. But there's something...compelling about it," Florence said after they'd stood side by side for several long moments.

"I have to agree with you. I didn't understand what your mother found so compelling about North Dakota and why she chose this state in which to settle, but...I feel it now." That was no lie. He understood completely why someone might be drawn to the compelling wildness of the open country.

"I'm lonely," Florence said softly beside him.

He didn't know what to say to that. He wasn't sure what exactly she meant. Thankfully, after a few heartbeats of silence, she spoke again, and he had to strain to hear her over the pounding of hammers and the calls of the men who were working behind them.

"I think... I just really liked singing last night, but it made me miss being a family. Or something. It gave me a longing for something else."

He could understand that. Maybe not exactly what she was saying, but as they sang, it almost made him somehow feel closer to Annika, but it also made him miss her more if that made sense. Like it pulled back the curtain and showed him that the hole in his life she left when she died was still there.

Not that he ever thought it would disappear, just that other things would fill up the area around it and it wouldn't be as noticeable at times.

"I just talked to Sebastian. He's going to start looking for nannies. We'll have someone here by the end of August."

His words didn't have the reaction he had hoped for. It almost looked like she deflated more than anything.

"You think you're too old for a nanny?" he asked, holding his breath and hoping that wasn't the case. He was the parent. He could tell her whether she was going to get a nanny or not, but usually Florence didn't fight him, and if she truly didn't want one, he wasn't sure he would make her, just because she was typically so easygoing.

"I want a family." She emphasized the last word. "Not someone who is hired to be with me."

He nodded. "I get it."

They didn't say anything else, and eventually they made their way back to the car and drove back to town, stopping at the diner to eat supper. He hadn't unpacked any kitchen utensils, and he wasn't a great cook anyway. They had someone cook meals for them back in Tennessee, as well as do light housekeeping, and Jones had figured he didn't need to learn.

His job had always been to sing. That's what he was good at. He wasn't even sure he was making a halfway decent dad.

# Chapter 5

"Why weren't you at school today?" Merritt asked, sitting at the kitchen table where Toni's mom had piled a big plate of cookies.

Toni hadn't even asked her to make them. They'd just gone out to the kitchen, cooked lunch together, and then her mom had suggested it.

Her mom had seemed to forget that she had thrown up earlier in the day and hadn't said anything when Toni had asked if her friends could come over and eat cookies and talk.

Or maybe she just felt bad. Or maybe she was trying to get Toni to forget that she walked in on her while she was crying.

Her mom was back upstairs in her office, continuing her job search.

Toni lowered her voice anyway, because she didn't want her to hear. "I need to find a husband for my mom, now."

"I thought you were going to let the Lord handle it?" Sorrell said, looking at Toni with her brows raised. Toni had been very adamant that that's what her mom wanted.

Toni knew it, and she figured her friends would want an explanation. "Mom was crying."

Her friends' eyes opened wide. And then they nodded.

"We'll have to work fast."

That's what Toni figured. No more explanation was necessary. She didn't even have to tell them that her mom lost her job.

"You know, I've been hearing a lot of things about Billy," Merritt said, sounding thoughtful.

Toni wanted to roll her eyes. She couldn't get the matchmakers to work. Charlene wouldn't give them her love potion. Even Miss April, who had taken over from Charlene, had been nothing but a flop. The Marry Me Chicken hadn't worked on her mom either. And they'd tried it twice.

"Mom is immune to any kind of matchmaking. Everything we've tried. Nothing has worked."

She knew she had just asked her friends to help her and then shot their ideas down, but she felt so discouraged. And desperate. She couldn't stand to see her mom crying.

Even if the crying was over a job, if she were married, she wouldn't have been crying. Her husband could have fixed everything. Because that's what husbands were for. To fix stuff.

"You can't give up before we even start." Sorrell shook her head. "Start for this time, I mean."

"I know your mom has been hard to match, but maybe if she's crying, that means she's softening."

"She lost her job," Toni said, not wanting her friends to get the wrong idea either.

"Good," Merritt said right away.

"Merritt!" Sorrell chided her sister.

"What? The guy she worked for was a jerk. I can't believe she put up with him for so long." She shrugged, and her facial expression said she didn't care what the others thought, she thought that was the best thing that could have happened to Toni's mom.

Toni supposed she should look at it like that too. But truth be told, she was a little scared. Her mom didn't always share a lot of info with her, but she did know that they needed that job.

"Mom said that we might have to move away if she can't find a job around here. That's the other reason why we need to find her a husband, now."

"And you deserve a dad," Sorrell said, and her tone was compassionate.

Toni looked down at the table. Apparently God hadn't thought she deserved a dad. She tried not to think like that, but that's the way it felt. Like He didn't think she was good enough or something.

She tried to tell herself that God actually thought she was good enough that she *didn't* need a dad. That she could just depend on God to be her Father. But sometimes the negative thoughts crept in, and she couldn't push them aside.

"All right. What prospects do we have?" Merritt said, shoving the rest of the cookie into her mouth and then folding her hands on the table like they were at an actual board meeting.

If she was chewing with her mouth closed, she would have made a more authoritarian-looking figure, but as it was, the partially chewed cookie in her mouth ruined the effect.

"There's some guy who just moved in beside us. And his niece, who lives with him, is going to go to school on Monday. She's our age."

"Really?" Merritt asked, with her brows raised.

Toni didn't want her to go off on a rabbit trail. "And I think the man is about Mom's age, but it's hard to tell."

"All right. That's our number one suspect."

"Prospect. Not suspect."

"Whatever. How can we get him to eat some Marry Me Chicken?" Merritt said, picking up a cookie, which Toni was pretty sure was her fourth. Not that Toni was keeping track. She'd already had six.

"The Marry Me Chicken doesn't work," Toni reminded them.

"We need Billy," Sorrell said, slapping her hand on the table, which made Toni put a finger to her lips and say "Shh!" then look over her shoulder like her mom would be coming down the stairs any second.

Sorrell grimaced. "Sorry. But we do!"

"That didn't work either. Billy already had a run-in with him yesterday, and he was hanging out at the front of his porch earlier this afternoon when they came home from wherever they went."

Toni tried not to sound too depressed. Even though she didn't really believe that Billy was a matchmaking steer, she had hoped when she had seen the man with him yesterday and then saw that they lived beside them. She'd been thrilled when he'd followed them to the porch, but...it was a big fat zero.

"You know what I think?" Merritt asked, lifting her brows and looking between her sister and her friend.

"What?" Toni asked, knowing when Merritt got a look like that, it usually involved something that would end up being successful.

"I think you need to go to that man yourself and ask him to marry your mom. Simple as that." She nodded her head as though she just delivered the Gettysburg Address for the first time and then looked rather proud of herself, like she wrote it, too.

"I can't go ask some man to marry my mom."

"Why not?" Merritt rewarded herself with another cookie and shoved the entire thing in her mouth.

Why couldn't she? She opened her mouth to give an excuse but couldn't think of one. The closest thing she could come up with was that he might say no.

She couldn't think of any other reason other than...it just wasn't done.

"You're a kid. You can get away with anything," Merritt said, lifting her brows as she reached for another cookie. Like that proved her point.

"I have to agree with Merritt," Sorrell said seriously. "What do you have to lose? He said he wasn't going to stay long. So, it's not like you're going to have to see him every day for the rest of your life if he says no. And he might say yes."

"But he hasn't even met my mom."

"But he sang with her. Sometimes music is good at bringing your emotions out," Merritt said. "I cry during sad songs."

Toni pulled her lip back but didn't say anything, thinking on it a little longer.

"All right. Fine. I'll do it." Why not? "I better do it before Mom comes down from her office. Because she is going to kill me if she finds out. You guys are not going to tell her." Toni lifted her brows at her friends. She hated keeping things from her mom. Her mom was always so nice and went out of her way to say yes as often as she could. Toni knew she'd been really blessed to have such a great mom. But this felt like something that was urgent, and... Maybe it put her a little bit in mind of the Marry Me Chicken. Where she had gone behind her mom's back trying to get someone to fall in love with her, and her mom got mad. This would definitely make her mom mad.

And embarrassed if she found out.

"Do you want us to stay in here and make sure that she doesn't go out if she comes downstairs?" Sorrell offered.

"No, that would just look weird that you guys are sitting here and I'm not around. I'll just do it right now, and we'll see what happens." Toni nodded her head. If she was going to do it, she needed to do it before she chickened out.

# Chapter 6

Dusk was settling down by the time Jones and Flo got back to the duplex.

He'd already promised Florence that they'd sit outside that evening and sing, but they had to get cleaned up from being on the ranch and he had a few calls to make.

He'd just finished a second call, and Florence was in the shower, when there was a knock at his door.

As long as it wasn't a steer trying to run him down again. That furry, horned one hadn't bothered them on the sidewalk, but Jones had looked out his window and seen him a couple of times.

Now that it was dark, he couldn't tell where he was.

But he was pretty sure the steer wouldn't knock.

He shoved his phone in his pocket, tilted his head to make sure that he could hear the shower running, and then opened the door.

Toni, the girl from next door, stood on the doorstep.

"Good evening. What's up?"

She looked very serious. "I need to talk to you." She paused for a moment and seemed to look over her shoulder.

It seemed odd that she gave a furtive glance over her shoulder, as though afraid she was being followed. Maybe she was afraid Billy was going to attack her. Although she hadn't seemed scared of the steer before when they were together. Maybe something happened.

"Can I come in?" she almost whispered.

"Of course." He opened the door and stood back, waiting for her to walk in, curious now as to what his brand-new neighbor could possibly want. Maybe, his heart stirred with hope, she wanted to hang out with Florence.

That would be awesome. Florence seemed down all day, and if playing with a friend would cheer her up, Jones was all for it.

The girl stopped and turned around and was staring straight at him as he shut the door behind him.

"Will you marry my mom?"

Jones's hand tightened on the doorknob behind him as he slumped back against the door.

His whole body seemed to jerk with an electrical shock.

He narrowed his eyes at the girl. She couldn't have said what he thought he heard.

But he couldn't think of anything else that her words could mean. How had he misheard them?

"I'm sorry?" he finally said, and his voice not only didn't sound like his, but it sounded like it was coming from a long distance away.

"Will you marry my mom?"

The girl repeated it word for word. Her face seemed stoic, but there was pleading in her eyes, maybe a desperation.

"Why?" he finally said, although that probably wasn't the best question to ask.

"She needs a husband."

"Why?"

"She's sad."

Well, he definitely wasn't going to ask this girl to play with Florence because she was sad if that was how she cheered people up.

"I...could sing to her." Which sounded funny even to his ears. After all, these people probably didn't know he was supposed to be a famous singer. But he'd rather sing to her than marry her...

"No. I mean, you can if you want to, but she needs a husband."

The girl didn't move. She just stood there staring at him. It was getting to be a little uncomfortable.

"I'm sorry. I...feel like maybe I missed something. I've never even met your mom. You can't just go around marrying people. You have to know them. Date them. Decide that you're in love with them, and then you think about whether or not you want to marry them. But that's...years away." He was just saying what he'd been taught all his life. What normal people did. Maybe people in North Dakota weren't normal. After all, they had wild steers running up and down the sidewalk accosting innocent newcomers.

"Couldn't you decide you have enough things in common? Or couldn't you decide that you'll take a chance on her?"

"I'm sorry. I can't marry your mom."

"Uncle Jones? That's a perfect solution."

Jones groaned in his soul. His eyes, slowly, fatalistically, moved to the stairs, where Flo descended one slow step at a time, dawning hope on her face. That hope made his heart sink even further, past his toes, drilling a hole into the floor at his feet.

"Florence."

"Uncle Jones. It's perfect. I don't need a nanny, we need a family. And I'll have a built-in friend." At that, his eyes went to Toni, who was staring at him with the same dawning hope on her face that Florence had on hers. They smiled at each other, their grins growing bigger and bigger until both of them turned back to him, beaming like it was Christmas morning.

"I'll be the best friend she ever had. I've always wanted a sister. Actually, I prayed more for a little brother, but I'll take a sister." Toni sounded like she was being very magnanimous in accepting a sister over a brother, but it was clear there was excitement in her voice.

"Does your mother know you're doing this?"

"She will agree to it," Toni said quickly, making him think that her mother had no idea what she was doing and probably wouldn't agree to it.

Hope sprang up in his breast. If he agreed, and she disagreed, he wouldn't look like the bad guy. It wouldn't be him that wiped the smiles off the faces of these girls, it would be her. He didn't even know her name!

But it didn't matter. No sane woman was going to marry some random guy she'd never even met. So, feeling rather pleased with himself, he allowed a smile to spread across his face.

"All right. I'll do it."

# Chapter 7

$M$allie rubbed her bleary eyes as she slowly descended the steps.

It was hard to imagine feeling more discouraged.

She had some correspondence from her old job, information on what to do with her health insurance and what to do if she wanted to file for unemployment, etc.

She thought that Samson would fight her on it, and she wasn't sure she wanted to go through that.

However, if her job search remained fruitless, she certainly would.

A little bit of unemployment was better than nothing.

As she reached the bottom of the stairs, the dulcet tones of the guitar from last night reached her ears.

No wonder she hadn't heard anything out of Toni. She could hear the harmony before she even opened the door.

Smiling at the old, familiar hymn they were singing, she stepped slowly out to the dark night.

There was slightly more light tonight than there had been the night before, enough for her to be able to see the outlines of the three different heads on her porch.

She felt caught up in the music, drawn to go sit with them, but her phone buzzed, and thinking it could be a job prospect, even at this hour of the night, she turned and walked back inside. It turned out that it was an old friend who had heard her news and called to chat, and Mallie never did make it back outside.

# Chapter 8

"Good morning, ladies," Mallie said as she walked into the community building Saturday morning.

An unexpected thunderstorm had come up the night before, and she'd ended up not going back out to the porch when she got off the phone.

Instead, Toni and she had snuggled down and watched a movie together. After that, they sat on opposite ends of the couch with their blanket, a candle burning cheerfully between them as they read until after midnight on their e-readers.

She'd always dreamed of having a daughter, and not necessarily of changing her clothes and making her look pretty, but of doing things like that. Spending time together, reading together, having cozy evenings together.

Of course, she always thought she'd have a husband to share those times with too.

Life hadn't worked out that way, and she had regrets, but they were pointless, so she tried not to dwell on them.

"Mallie! We heard you had a new neighbor," Miss April said, looking up from where she was sorting quilting squares at the table in front of her.

Miss June sat at a different table, putting a flower arrangement together, and Miss Helen was there as well, doing some kind of needlepoint work.

"Yes, a man and his niece. Toni's talked to them, but I haven't. Not yet." She should make a casserole or something to welcome them.

"Take some food over and introduce yourself," Miss April said with a smile. "I heard he's single."

"He is?" Mallie asked, as though the thought hadn't occurred to her at all. She was pretty sure he was single. She hadn't seen a wife.

"That's what we heard. We haven't quite gotten all of his information out. He seems to be...playing things close to the vest. I have heard that he's related to someone famous. I don't know whether it's true or not," Miss April said as she put a blue piece of fabric on top of the pile of blue fabric she already had.

Mallie hadn't really come in to talk about her neighbor, although she wasn't going to turn down any information on him. Any man who would sit outside, playing guitar and singing with his niece, was someone she would consider a nice man and wouldn't mind getting to know better. Even if it was just on a friendship level. Which was all she felt ready for right now. Considering she had no job.

That was what she was here to talk to the ladies about.

"We had a warm spring so far. And dry. This could be a hot summer," Miss Helen said, shaking her head.

If Mallie was a farmer, that information would probably be considered bad news. But she loved the heat, especially after the cold North Dakota winter, and she was ready to be warm all the time.

"We had a pretty wet year last year, from what I understand, so it makes sense that we get some dry years too," Mallie said, never knowing what to say when people talked about the weather. It seemed like such a silly thing to discuss. The weather was going to do what it was going to do, and there wasn't anything she was going to be able to do about it.

"So what brings you in here this morning?" Miss June asked, as though she could tell that Mallie wasn't overly comfortable with the weather discussion.

"I was hoping you all might help me."

"We'd love to!" Miss April said immediately, without having to think about it.

That was one of the things Mallie had loved about the small town. Everybody was always so willing to pitch in with anything that needed to be done. It made her feel like she belonged, even though she was fairly new, only having been here for a few years.

"I lost my job. I've applied everywhere online I can think of, and I'd really like to get something to tide me over until I can pick something else up."

"Aren't you getting unemployment?" Miss June asked.

"I should be. But...my boss isn't always the kindest person, and the last I spoke with him, he gave me the feeling that he was going to fight me on it. So if I'm going to get it, I'm going to have to go to court for it. I really don't want to do that."

"I've heard they usually rule in favor of the employee, as long as you have even a modicum of proof that you were let go without notice through no fault of your own," Miss Helen said, pushing the needle through the material.

"I've heard that too, but... I just hate the idea of going to court and arguing about it. I'd rather be working anyway. So, that's what I'm going to try to do if I can. Obviously, if I can't, I'll wait for whatever I can get. Just because I have to feed my daughter and keep a roof over her head."

She tried not to let panic sit down in her chest. Not the idea that she would take care of her daughter, but that it was just her, that if anything happened to her, if she was unable to get a job and take care of Toni, scared her more than anything.

Well, maybe more than anything except what would happen to Toni if she got sick or, God forbid, died.

She needed Toni to be taken care of.

That thought had always been in the back of her head, especially since Toni's dad was not in the picture, nor did he want to be, but now that she lost her job, it had become something that nagged at her thoughts, and if she didn't get a hold of it, she could lay awake at night worrying about it. She needed to have someone that she could depend on, who would make sure that Toni was okay if anything happened to her.

"What work did you do?" Miss June asked, compassion in her tone and concern in her gaze as she looked up from her flowers.

"I was an administrative assistant. I know that means different things to different people, but it was a virtual position, where I did all of my work online and had video calls when necessary. It didn't require me to go to the office at all. I'd really like to be able to keep working from home."

"Maybe God shut this down because he has a new direction that he wants you to go," Miss April said, her hands moving over the fabric. She never looked up, but her words held wisdom.

Mallie had thought of that. That maybe the Lord wanted her to shift her focus, shift her direction. But that was scary. She didn't want to do anything differently. She wanted to keep being able to make ends meet, support her daughter, and not have the scary black opening in front of her, feeling like one misstep and she was going to fall into an endless gaping pit from which she could never return.

She wasn't quite sure why the future felt like that to her right now, other than she allowed her fear to take root and start growing.

"You know, God sometimes works that way. He takes what seems like a terrible thing—a job loss—and turns it into the best thing that ever happened to us in our entire lives." Miss April spoke casually, but Mallie noticed Miss June was watching her.

She heard rumors around town that Miss June's husband had cheated. She didn't usually give credence to rumors, especially when she'd overheard someone just mentioning it and didn't know for sure what the circumstances were or whether the person who was talking really knew what they were talking about. Still, she wondered from the look on Miss June's face if maybe she was thinking a little harder about what Miss April said because she had reached a turning point of her own and needed to make some decisions.

The idea that other people were in, if not exactly her same position, but at least one similar, made Mallie feel a little bit better.

Everyone faced these small crises in their lives. It was how she responded to it that would show her character.

She wanted there to be some kind of substance in her character, but she could just never be sure.

Until she was tested. Now was the time to see what she was really made of. Whether she would turn to the Lord, or whether she would crumble and allow her fear to overcome.

"I guess if God opens a door, I'll walk through it."

"You guess?" Miss April asked with a lifted brow, holding one green square of material in her hand.

"I'll try. Sometimes it seems like God asks us to do really hard things."

"Sometimes those things are scary, but they turn out to be the very best things."

She couldn't argue with Miss Helen and simply nodded her head.

The ladies were right. Sometimes the door opened and what she saw on the other side looked scary and hard, and she didn't want to keep walking. But if she didn't walk through, she would miss out on the opportunities God wanted her to have.

She determined in her heart that she would keep her mind open to whatever opportunities God placed in her path and that she wouldn't say no if she was sure it was the Lord.

*Lord, help me to be brave. Give me courage to do what You want me to do. Please be clear about it, because I can be dense sometimes.*

She whispered the prayer as the door in the community center opened and Lark Stryker, the veterinarian who also had a girls' home outside of Sweet Water, walked in.

"Good morning, ladies," Lark said, her gaze encompassing the room.

"Good morning, Lark. We were just talking about God opening doors."

"And there I am, opening the door." Lark laughed.

"I wasn't suggesting that you were the Lord," Miss April chided Lark.

"Oh, trust me. I know no one is going to get confused about that," Lark said, stepping into the community building and closing the door behind her.

"Oh, Lark, how do you always manage to be so happy?" Miss June said, holding a flower in her hand and smiling at Lark.

Mallie could echo her question. Lark always seemed to have a smile on her face and a positive attitude.

"Well, you're talking about walking through the doors God opens. I guess that's what you need to do, just smile and assume that God has the very best in store for you. Kinda hard to be gloomy when you're constantly thinking about all the good things that God is going to do."

Mallie wanted to roll her eyes at herself, because Lark's words were so simple yet so profound. How could she be worried or scared when she believed God was exactly what He said He was—always good, always loving, always kind. Always wanting the best for her.

But she looked around the suffering in the world and wondered if God was going to want her to go through that, and it scared her and made her forget that God was always good.

"That's such a good point," she said to Lark who had walked over, carrying a small package.

"It's not always easy to remember though," Lark said, her brows raised and her tone saying that she totally understood what Mallie was saying. "Miss June, I have the flea and tick pills you need for your cats. They came in the mail yesterday, but I didn't get a chance to ride in until this morning."

Lark took the medicine over while Mallie said good day to everyone and walked out. They hadn't helped her find a job, but they had given her information that was going to be helpful. She needed to keep her chin up and remember that whatever the Lord had planned for her, it was going to be good. She just needed to walk through the door He opened.

# Chapter 9

Jones held the door open for Florence, then stepped out on the front porch behind her.

Friday night, a thunderstorm had blown up unexpectedly, which had driven them into the house before Toni's mom had come out.

Saturday, they had been at the ranch and had gotten home late.

Work on the ranch had been coming along faster than he expected, and they might not be at the duplex much longer.

Which meant that if he was going to keep his word to Florence, he would need to ask the neighbor lady, whom he had yet to meet, to marry him very soon.

What had seemed like a really great idea as he had been standing and listening to Florence tell him how she wanted a mother and a friend had gone from sounding a little bit crazy but doable to sounding completely crazy, and he wasn't quite sure why he had even agreed to it.

The woman was going to think he was nuts. But that was kind of what he wanted. He would do what Florence had asked, he would look like a great uncle, and the woman would be the one who would have to break her heart. Not Jones.

He tried to remind himself of that when his stomach cramped as they walked outside.

Tried to remind himself he wasn't nervous. He was expecting, no, hoping, to get turned down.

Just... How did you start a conversation like that?

Hold out his hand, introduce himself, and then tack on a, "Will you marry me?" at the end?

He was going to have to come up with something fast though, because as he turned to look across the divider between their two porches, the woman and her daughter were already sitting on their porch swing.

He should have come out earlier. He would have had more time to prepare.

Summoning his most charming smile, he walked over to the divider.

There had been a reason why he had sung backup and his sister had been the lead in their band.

He hadn't even been mentioned, her name had been the star name, and he had gladly taken a back seat to her. He never wanted to be in the spotlight. Always happy helping someone else succeed.

No matter how many times Annika had prodded him, saying that he was just as talented as she was and just as capable, he'd always wanted all the accolades to point to her so he could have peace and quiet and blend into the background.

"Good evening. I was hoping you'd be out here this evening," he said, surprised that his voice actually sounded normal.

The woman smiled when she saw him and got up off the swing. She walked over with her hand out. He was surprised that she was, maybe not beautiful, exactly, but a sweet-looking woman, with bright eyes and a cheerful smile.

"I was hoping to see you as well. I'm Mallie."

"Jones," he said, holding his hand out.

Her brows went up a little, as though thinking that he had given her his last name. He'd gotten that response more than once when he introduced himself to people, and he was used to it.

"That's my first name."

She huffed out a bit of a laugh. A typical reaction. "I wondered. I thought maybe you were introducing yourself with your last name.

But then I thought maybe it was just a nickname or something. You know how some people just go by their last name or some short form of it like Mac."

"Yeah. I get that all the time. I have no idea what my parents were thinking, but I've been saddled with it all my life, and I'm used to people being a little bit confused when I introduce myself."

"All right. So my reaction was normal."

Her hand was soft in his, but her grip was firm. And her eye contact easy.

She didn't drill him with her eyes, but there was a laughing kind of glow about her.

The small lines at the corners of her eyes spoke of age, but they also spoke of laughter and fun and the fact that she wasn't afraid to have either. He liked them. Liked that she wasn't as young as she sounded and that her face had a little bit of age and wisdom to it.

He found himself wondering what it might be like if he wasn't going to ask her to marry him and just...struck up a relationship with her.

It had been years since he'd had time to do that. Touring with his sister, managing the band, writing songs, producing them, and then with the work on the ranch, he hadn't had time to pursue any type of relationship.

He was also very distrustful of women who pursued him. He'd seen too many people in his position have women go after them just because of their fame and money.

He didn't want to make that same mistake and have his marriage not last. Or his relationship crumble because it was based on su-perficial things that faded with time.

Fame for sure, and money if not wisely managed, and some-times even then.

Florence had moved from behind him, and she and her friend were whispering over the divider. They giggled and went to the stairs, where they put their arms around each other and whispered.

That strengthened his resolve. To see them getting along so well, to know that he was going to do something that could possibly help his niece or at least make her feel very grateful toward him.

"I'm glad to see Toni has a new friend. Sweet Water is such a friendly town, but it's nice to have someone right beside us," Mallie said, smiling at the girls.

He turned back to her. "Will you marry me?"

That was poorly done.

Some people had the gift of gab, some people didn't. He didn't. There had probably been a hundred different ways to lead up to that, and maybe if Annika was still alive, she could have helped him. But he'd always seen things more in black and white and didn't like to manipulate people, and buttering them up before he gave them an unsuspected punch definitely seemed like manipulation to him.

Mallie's eyes grew wide, and her mouth dropped.

She blinked, and with each flutter of her eyelids, his heart did backward somersaults while his stomach covered its eyes and shook its head.

Well, she didn't have to worry about him flirting with other women. Since obviously, his ability to be romantic was sadly lacking. Maybe it wasn't that he didn't have time to foster a relationship, maybe it was more that he didn't have the skills.

He was able to sing, and that was usually how his emotions came out.

"You know what—" he began.

She put her hand up. "Yes. I will."

She smiled. And he took a step back. He couldn't help it; she was supposed to say no.

He was going to give her an out. Say something about him being a little bit crazy, and she could turn him down, it wasn't a big deal. Maybe he'd even explain to her that he was only doing it because Florence had asked him to. She wanted a sister, and he knew she was lonely and she lost her mom and he actually needed someone to watch her and all that.

"You said yes?"

"Yes." She laughed a little, like she could hardly believe she had. "Would you believe that I've been thinking about and praying about how I need to walk through any door that the Lord opens for me. It is actually something that I've been telling myself, almost chanting to myself over and over again this weekend. I...lost my job last week."

"Oh. I'm sorry."

He hadn't known. Hadn't suspected at all.

"Yeah. Thursday actually. When we sang together. That...made things easier on my heart. It just calmed me some and made me realize that God is in control. I was still fighting it Saturday though. Because my job search hadn't been going very well. I spoke to some ladies at the community center, and they reminded me that sometimes God has these things happen in our lives so that we can become stronger. So that we can grow. So that God can open a new door, and we just have to not be afraid to walk through it."

"I see." She could be talking about Annika's death. He had to do a lot of things he wasn't comfortable with after his sister died. Raising his niece on his own for one. Learning to sing again, for another. Being the front person in the band. The one that everyone was looking at. He had been dreading that, even as he'd been telling his agent that he was getting ready to write songs and go back out. He knew the world wanted to see him, but he'd always been able to stand behind Annika.

He nodded his head. "That's definitely something that I need to do as well. Not to be afraid of the challenges that God puts in front of me. So often, I get scared and want to use common sense, or what feels like common sense, to say no."

"Exactly. The common sense that says when a strange man you just met today asks you to marry him, say no." She grimaced a little, still smiling. "Maybe that's a smart thing to do, except... It just seems like God had been preparing me for this. Are you serious?" She added the last part in a disbelieving tone like she just had to make sure.

"I was. I know this isn't going to sound very romantic, but Florence needs a nanny. I had told her that I would be looking for one, and she told me that I needed to get married. She asked me if I would marry you." He paused, then figured he might as well continue. "Her mother died not that long ago, just a year. I'm the uncle stepping in. While I've always had a great relationship with her, and in some ways it was a father-type relationship, I'm a little uncomfortable in the role. Still. And so I didn't want to say no to her."

"So you said you'd ask, assuming that I would say no?" Mallie said, grinning as though she understood exactly where he was coming from. "Then I would be the bad guy."

He chuckled, guilty.

"Isn't it nice whenever somebody else can play the role of the bad guy and you as a parent doesn't have to?"

"It seems like all I do is say no and make her do things that she doesn't want to."

"Same."

They shared sympathetic looks at each other, over their shared struggle as parents, finding it funny that they both understood how difficult it was to be the right kind of parent, the kind of parent to set boundaries for their child and then enforce them. And how nice it was when someone else could enforce those boundaries for them.

"So... Would you really do it?" he asked, looking into her eyes and trying to read her expression. She didn't look like the kind of woman who just did random things like that, and he definitely wasn't that kind of man. But...

"Well, sounds like you need someone to help you take care of Florence, Toni would love to have a sister, and I told the Lord I would walk through whatever door he opened for me. So…" She shrugged her shoulders. "I'm in. But if you think it's too crazy, I totally understand."

"I don't think it's so crazy as much as I think… Marriage is forever. It's not just something to play with."

"I agree. I… I was married once before, and he didn't feel that way. I haven't wanted to take the plunge again. Just because I had no idea that he was the kind of person who didn't take commitment seriously."

A sound from one of the girls made them turn their heads and look down the steps.

"That's the steer that chased me down the sidewalk last week. The first day I was here."

"Billy chased you?"

"Maybe not chased exactly, but he walked after me, and those horns—"

"Yeah, they are pretty big. But Billy is just a big pushover. We use him for the children when we have festivals. They like to take turns petting him and sitting on him, and someone was trying to teach him to lead so that we could lead him around with a kid on his back. He's…just a big sweetheart. I promise if he was following you, it wasn't with any kind of evil intentions in mind."

"That's what everyone else has said too. But I just had a hard time believing it. After all, those horns."

They laughed together.

Then they sobered, still watching the girls pet Billy, while Toni seemed to be telling Florence all about him. They couldn't hear the words, since they were spoken rather low, but it looked like Toni was showing Florence where to scratch him.

"So we agreed that we both think marriage is forever. So, while this is a little unconventional, it's not like we have to do things the way the rest of the world does. In fact, if we get married and stay married, that would be a little bit unique."

"Wouldn't it?" Mallie grunted. "Yeah. I... I'm totally open to the idea. I am a little bit scared thinking about it, and I wouldn't mind talking a little bit more about it, but I am good to go. I told God I would walk through the door, this seems to be it, so whatever you want. I'm open for the next move."

"All right. It's Sunday night. I have to take Florence to school in the morning and get her registered for classes. I don't think that'll take very long, and then I needed to go out to the ranch. I've been trying to supervise things, that seems to make things flow a little bit better."

He didn't mention that he was going to try to get some writing time in as well. His agent had been very patient and given him an entire year to get used to being without Annika. It was time for him to get moving on his songs again.

"I have to watch Brooklyn's twins tomorrow. She'll be dropping them off about the time Toni leaves for school. I can get them settled, and I'll be ready to go whenever you come back? Or I can drive out myself."

"No. Let's go in one car. I'll drive to school, get Florence registered, then I'll come back and pick up you and the twins. How old are they?" He assumed they weren't school-age, but babies might be a little bit more difficult than toddlers or preschoolers. Not that he had any more experience other than Florence with any age group.

"They're three. So, we don't have to make sure they don't put anything in their mouth, but we will have to keep an eye on them, especially if we're out at the ranch."

"There aren't any animals at the ranch yet. My sister had visions for it overflowing with animals and maybe even being a dude ranch. Someplace where people could come out and hang out."

"There's already a dude ranch going up in Sweet Water. I'm sure a second one could only make it better."

He'd have to tell her his connection to his famous sister and explain that there might be more of a draw than just a dude ranch for him. Or maybe he'd just like it to be a private residence. If... If he was actually going to get married to this woman, they'd need to talk about it.

"That should give us the day with some privacy, beyond the twins, to talk about things."

"That sounds good. If we're going to do it, we should be able to discuss it, decide if we are truly doing what the Lord wants us to do, and then move forward. There's no point in getting stuck in endless questions and trying to decide whether or not we're going forward."

"I agree completely."

"Are we going to sing tonight? I think Billy came just because he wants to hear us." Florence turned around and looked at him with pleading eyes.

"That's the look I can never say no to," he said as an aside to Mallie.

"I totally understand," Mallie said as an aside right back to him.

"We're going to sing, Mom? That's why we came out."

He smiled, thinking that maybe Mallie had enjoyed singing with him as much as he had enjoyed singing with her. There hadn't been too many people in his life that had seemed to fit him quite like Annika, which wasn't surprising considering that Annika was his sister and they grew up together. What was surprising was that a perfect stranger, someone he couldn't even see in the darkness, had harmonized so well with him.

"I see what you're thinking, and it's true. We came out for the express purpose of hoping to sing with our neighbors again," Mallie said with a smile.

"All right. Then I wouldn't want to let anyone down, not just Florence." His eyes twinkled at hers. She grinned, understanding that he was basically saying that he didn't want to tell her no any more than he wanted to tell Florence no.

The thought definitely seemed to make her happy, and for some reason, he couldn't keep the smile off his face either.

He was a little nervous about the next day. Nervous because he'd never done something so crazy in his entire life. The life of a singer superstar seemed to be a lot of luck and overnight success, but it really wasn't. He and Annika had spent a lot of time perfecting their harmonies, working on the instruments they played, and playing every time they'd been given an opportunity, judging crowd reactions, and writing more songs that were crowd pleasers, hoping for their big break. Being an overnight success involved a lot of years of hard work.

He had a feeling that, possibly, his personal big break was just about ready to happen.

He hadn't even known he wanted one.

# Chapter 10

What had she done?

Mallie stood on the front porch, her arms wrapped around herself, her eyes staring unseeing off into the darkness.

The clop of hooves on the sidewalk made her turn her head, and a shaggy figure strolled blearily into sight.

She moved from the far corner over to the stairs.

It was Billy, coming back around after listening to them sing for a while earlier in the evening.

Everyone had dispersed around ten, and they went inside to go to bed.

Only Mallie couldn't sleep.

"Am I crazy?" she whispered to the steer as she ran her hands down his neck and then scratched behind his ears.

He shook his head side to side, wanting her to scratch harder and more area, but it looked like he was shaking his head no.

"I feel like I'm crazy."

What kind of woman said yes to marry a man she just met that day?

She had sworn when Toni's father walked out that she would not marry again.

In the back of her head, she thought that if she did, they would date for a million years first, so she would know every single thing about him and wouldn't be blindsided by the fact that he couldn't keep his eyes off other women, and that he couldn't keep a commitment to save his life, and that he lied like a rug.

She swallowed down the bitterness. Happy thoughts. She needed to be thankful that she had Toni. That was the one good thing that had come out of her disastrous relationship with her ex.

That, and she felt like she was a wiser person than she was previously.

But now, she wasn't so sure.

She just said yes to a question that bound her into an unbreakable commitment. Technically, she was engaged.

She didn't give commitments easily, because she liked to be able to keep her word.

She wanted to be able to do what she said she was going to do, to be dependable, to have people know that when she gave her word, it meant something.

After all, she had very little money, so her integrity, her word, her character were really all she had as commodities.

And she didn't typically buy or sell them.

But she felt a little bit like she had this evening. After all, the man was looking for a nanny, and she had exchanged her...freedom? She wasn't sure if that was the right word, but maybe she should have said that she would be a nanny, rather than a wife.

That was far less commitment. And there was much greater room for her to step out if things didn't work out.

But wasn't that the problem in marriages? Things didn't work out, so people left.

Except, that's not what happened to her. Her husband had cheated.

If he hadn't left, she probably would have left him. Did she want to be married to a man who cheated and didn't keep his word? Especially when he didn't show any remorse and blamed her.

Maybe if he'd have apologized, they could have worked things out. Maybe if he had been willing to go to whatever lengths it took to let her know that he wasn't going to be doing it again.

But he hadn't even begun to come close to doing anything like that.

So therefore, she was left with little choice. She couldn't stay with a man she couldn't trust, and he wasn't concerned about, didn't care, whether she trusted him or not. But he had walked away. So therefore, the decision hadn't been hers.

She felt like she was rolling back all of the strides she had made and agreeing to marry someone she didn't even know.

Except... A man who sang with his niece in the evening on their porch. Who sang hymns. The old hymns. Who knew all the words. Something in her heart just told her that the kind of man who did that was the kind of man who would stay in his marriage. Who wouldn't cheat. Who would be honest and sincere.

Plus, of all the things that had been happening to her, and the advice that she had just been given to walk through the open door. It seemed crazy that she had just decided to do that, and then God opened an amazing opportunity right up in front of her.

How could she not walk through when she had determined that she would?

"Billy, I think I'm really going to do it."

Somehow, petting the animal soothed her, made her less anxious and more excited about the future. She wasn't sure exactly what it was, but as she brushed her hands off and turned to walk back up the stairs, she had a new determination in her heart that she would go in tomorrow to their conversation with an open mind. And with an excited eye on the future.

# Chapter 11

The twins came just after Toni got on the bus. Brooklyn was totally fine with her taking them anywhere and set the car seats on her porch since Jones wasn't there. He was still at the school enrolling Florence.

Brooklyn said they usually went down for a nap around one, but it would be fine if they didn't get one. Brooklyn wanted her to just integrate the kids into her day and not make her world revolve around them.

"Sometimes that's just the way things go, and kids need to understand that they're not the center of the universe," Brooklyn said with a laugh.

For having twins, Mallie had to admire her for looking so happy and energetic.

Sometimes just one child was more than she could handle. She had no idea how people with two did it.

She supposed when God gave that trial, he gave you the strength to do it.

Regardless, after Brooklyn left, Mallie was thankful that the twins were a boy and a girl, Evangeline and Eli. She wasn't sure whether she would have been able to tell two of the same gender apart.

"All right, you guys are gonna have fun today, right?" she asked as they looked longingly at the door after their mom.

They stood shoulder to shoulder, almost as though being side by side gave them strength.

"Your mom said you didn't eat breakfast yet. You want some eggs with cheese?"

"Eggs?" Eli said, his eyes brightening.

"I might even be able to find some bacon in the refrigerator."

"Yeah!" they said.

And just like that, they smiled and ran into the kitchen.

She thought they were going to sit down at the table or something, and she was going to suggest they play while she cooked, but they were dragging chairs over to the stove, and she realized after a couple of seconds that they were expecting to help.

Well, she could roll with that. Right?

"Do you guys help your mom a lot?" she asked, and they nodded their heads eagerly.

She supposed that was a really good idea and tried to think back as to what age Toni was when Mallie had started letting her help with the stove. Maybe not quite that young.

Regardless, she got the eggs out and a bowl and let each kid crack two into a bowl.

She figured she would eat two, and then she wondered whether she should make some for Jones.

She hadn't thought about that for very long when there was a knock on the door.

"Come in!" she called from the kitchen, not wanting to leave the twins by themselves.

"Hey!" Jones said as he walked in. "It didn't take nearly as long as I thought it was going to."

"That's good. Did Flo look like she was going to be okay?"

"Actually, Toni somehow got out of class and was hanging out with her the whole time. I guess she volunteered to show her around. So Florence was all smiles when I walked out."

"That's great. This is Evangeline," Mallie said, pointing to the little girl to her right. "And this is Eli. They're helping me make breakfast, and I was just wondering if you wanted us to make you some eggs."

"Sure. I'll take three."

"That's great. I have some bacon in the refrigerator, but I kinda got blindsided when they decided to help with the eggs, and haven't gotten it in the skillet."

"I can cook that," Jones said, with his brows raised, as though he was asking permission.

"That would be wonderful," Mallie said, more than a little surprised. She wasn't used to cooking in the kitchen with a man. Her ex had thought it was a woman's place to take care of the house, and he never helped with anything.

She didn't really mind, because before he left, that had been her only job. Still, it was frustrating to work all day and then continue to work after he got home, with him acting like she hadn't done anything, and it was her job to just serve him.

She often had to remind herself that Christ had called her to be a servant. It was one thing to choose to make the choice to be a servant, it was another thing to have her husband force her into the position.

Regardless, she shook those thoughts away and just tried to focus on the twins and how good it felt to have someone giving her a hand.

Those days were far away and long ago, and she supposed they probably taught her how good it was to have someone who was willing to help. Taught her to appreciate that.

They chatted with the kids as they cooked breakfast, and Mallie had to admit it was fun. Once her husband had left, she had been busy trying to earn a living, and while she enjoyed Toni's young years, she always felt the weight of responsibility on her shoulders and wished at times she could go back and just enjoy her child, rather than be constantly worrying about whether she was going to get her bills paid or not.

The Lord had provided everything they needed, and while Mallie had worked as hard as she could, God had never let her down.

With her newfound knowledge, she would have enjoyed her life a lot more.

They had breakfast on the table and the kids sitting in their seats before long.

Jones sat at the end of the table opposite from her, the kids on either side of them.

"Do you want me to say the blessing?" he asked, when she had settled herself after pouring drinks for everyone.

"Please," she said, trying not to show her surprise.

She smiled the whole time he spoke, listening and appreciating the fact that it was something he'd assumed that they were going to do.

Maybe God was trying to ease her mind, to tell her the decision she made had been the right one. She'd asked Him for a sign to let her know for sure. It felt like everything that had happened that morning had been things that had said to her, *this is okay. He's a good man.*

They put the dirty dishes in the dishwasher, and Mallie wiped off the table while Jones helped the kids down from their chairs and wiped their fingers and faces.

He acted like a man who had been around children before, and she wanted to ask how long he had been raising his niece.

But she figured they would have plenty of time to talk about those things, and so she kept the conversation light.

"Are you ready to go?" he asked as she finished wiping the table and rinsing the rag out in the sink.

"I think we are. I think you probably saw the car seats sitting on the porch as you walked in."

"I did. And I went ahead and put them in the back seat of my pickup before I came in."

"Oh. That's great."

"Are we going to see Mom?" Eli asked, looking up at the adults who were talking above his head.

"I have a ranch outside of town. There aren't any animals on it, but there are lots of people building things, and I thought we'd go out and take a look at them." He lifted his brows as though wanting to know what Eli thought. "Is that okay with you?"

"Loud noises make my ears hurt," Evangeline said, clutching a baby doll she brought and left on the couch while they ate.

"I don't think there are too many loud noises, but there might be some hammering going on. For the most part, it will just be men walking around and putting things together."

"I want to see it!" Eli said, looking at his sister with pleading on his face. "Come on, Evi. You'll be okay. I'll hold your hand."

His little three-year-old chest puffed out like he felt important that his sister needed him.

"Okay. But if it gets loud, can I leave?" Evangeline asked, her little nose scrunched up.

"I don't really like loud noises either. How about if it gets loud, you and I will both leave?" Mallie said, smiling at the little girl.

She nodded her head and then slipped her hand into Mallie's, which made Mallie's heart squeeze. Maybe it was the trust she showed or just the way being connected from one human to another made her heart feel light and happy. She wasn't sure. But she liked it.

It didn't take them long to get the kids buckled in the back. But as they climbed in the front seat, Jones said, "I didn't realize it was going to be so hot today. I should have told you that the air conditioning has gone out of my truck. I would have suggested you drive, but I needed to take the stuff that's in the back out. I grabbed it at the hardware store this morning on the way home from school."

"I don't mind. After such a long, cold winter, I'm always ready to be hot. Even more than hot. It won't bother me at all." She turned around to look at the kids. "You guys mind if we have our windows down?"

Evangeline shook her head no, but Eli nodded eagerly yes. She assumed that that meant he was eager to have the window down and didn't mind, just was answering a question slightly different than what she asked. Regardless, she figured she'd clarify. "So you like the window down?" she asked Eli.

"Yeah! I like to feel the wind."

His comment made Jones's head turn, and they shared a smile between them.

There was something sweet and warm, something that stirred her heart and made it beat slow and easy. Maybe it was just the feeling of family or the idea that they shared some communication without words. Or maybe it was just the cuteness of the children or the beauty of the hot spring day.

Whatever it was, Mallie felt happy to be alive, and although the worries about her income and what she was going to do hadn't completely disappeared, for the first time, she felt like maybe it was a good thing she had lost her job.

After all, if she hadn't gotten fired, she wouldn't be enjoying a day with two cute kids and the kind of man who seemed too good to be true.

The kind of man she had agreed to marry.

The thoughts sobered her.

"What's that look for?" Jones asked, glancing over at her as he backed out of the small parking area beside the house.

"I was just thinking what a really nice day it is. How I was so happy that I lost my job. I mean, that doesn't mean that I'm not still worried about things, but it just means that I can appreciate what I have right now, without having any expectations for the future. Or..." She laughed a little. "Not a whole lot of expectations, anyway."

"Expectations have a tendency to leave us disappointed."

"Oh, isn't that the truth?" she said, more fervently than what she meant to. She'd been burned so many times by things she expected to have happen.

"You probably expected to have air-conditioning on the way out to the ranch today. That one bit ya."

She laughed. "I hadn't even thought about air-conditioning. I honestly am just hoping that we get there and back and I haven't lost any children, and preferably with no blood or broken bones."

"You have high expectations for the day."

"Right? Maybe I should just let my expectations go and prepare for an emergency room visit."

"That would be a good idea. Considering neither one of us have much experience in ranch life, and we're used to one kid at a time."

They motored out of town, with him explaining to her where the ranch was and approximately how long it was going to take to get there. She was fine with whatever it was. Although she wondered if maybe she should have offered to pack a lunch. She hadn't even thought about it. But it was too late now, so she never said anything.

They had been driving for about ten minutes when there was a big bang, the truck bounced, and Jones said, "I think we just blew a tire. Hold on, let me try to get it to the side of the road and off the road."

# Chapter 12

J ones wanted to slap his hand on the steering wheel. Of all the times for his tire to blow out, it had to be now, when he had two small children and the woman whom he may or may not be going to marry sometime soon.

He almost laughed at the way the thoughts were going in his head. He really had no idea.

"I'm glad to see you're not upset," Mallie said, looking across the seat at him.

"Well, I admit that I thought I would have preferred for this to happen some other time, but my thoughts were just going in a completely different direction. I really wasn't laughing at our situation."

"I'm okay with that. I would rather you be happy than angry," Mallie said easily. "I can help you if you want me to. I've actually changed two tires along the road in the last few years. You'd think I'd have learned with the first one, but I didn't."

"Yeah. I think I ran over something. I didn't see it until we were on it, but it looked like something lying on the road punctured it. I can change it, but it will probably be an hour or so, and it's pretty hot for the kids to be sitting in the truck."

If it had happened a few minutes ago, when they were back on the main road, someone would probably have seen them and stopped to help. As it was, they'd just turned down a side road and they could go for several hours without a car going by.

"That's not a problem. I'll get them out, and we'll hang out here. I'm sure we can find something to do."

"I'm sorry," he offered, knowing that there really wasn't anything he could do, but he felt like he needed to apologize anyway.

"Don't worry about it. It's not your fault. I was thinking that I should have asked if you wanted me to pack a lunch or something. If I had done that, we could have had a picnic. Although, we just ate and I'm not the slightest bit hungry."

"I'm hungry," Eli offered from the back seat.

"How can you be hungry? We just ate?" Evangeline said, sounding like she was imitating something her mother had said a million times.

That made Jones laugh, and he looked over to see Mallie smiling too.

"All right. Then we won't get upset about it; we'll just get out and get it done."

"Perfect," she said and yanked on the door handle.

As he got the things he would need to change the tire out, she got the kids out of the truck and took them over to the side of the road. She started playing tag with them, and they were laughing and having a good time. It was nice music to listen to as he worked on getting the truck tire changed. It also made him think along the same lines as he'd been thinking all morning. She'd been pretty easygoing, having the kids standing at the counter helping her make breakfast, totally chill with him getting her skillet out and using it to fry bacon.

He'd been around some women who were very particular about their stove and about how much mess a person made, about their utensils and who could use them. She hadn't seemed the slightest bit concerned about things, and whatever he had done had been good enough. She hadn't insisted that she needed to do it herself so it got done right. He appreciated that about her.

He also appreciated that she wasn't upset about the delay or the setback. She wasn't worried about it and didn't get anxious or angry.

She just rolled with it. That was the kind of person he needed beside him. Someone who could handle his crazy schedules and roll with whatever happened.

Maybe the marriage thing wasn't such a crazy idea. Maybe she was right and God really had opened that door, because he certainly never considered proposing marriage to a virtual stranger before, and he definitely never thought she would say yes.

Eli came over after a little bit and squatted down beside him.

"Don't get too close, you don't want to get in the way, but you can watch how he does it. When you get older, you'll be able to do it yourself," Mallie said, scrunching down behind Eli, with Evangeline holding onto her neck and her arm around Evangeline's waist.

"Can I help?" Eli asked eagerly.

Jones tried to think of something he could do that would make him feel like he was helping and important.

"Well, you could hold these for me." He pointed to the lug nuts that he'd removed. "Once I changed a tire, and I lost one. I couldn't find it anywhere, and I hadn't done anything. It just...walked away."

"Really?" Eli asked, his eyes big.

"Well, probably not really. I don't think they have legs. Do you think?" Jones asked, hiding a smile as Eli picked one up and examined it.

"No. I don't think so."

"I didn't think so either. But it felt like it did, because I couldn't find it. And I don't know what else could have happened to it. So, maybe you could make sure that I don't lose any. How many do you have?" he asked as Eli carefully counted them.

"You missed one, Eli!" Evangeline said, pointing at one that lay off to the side.

The twins were involved, also keeping the hubcap from walking away, and it almost felt like a family affair as they finished changing the tire together.

He hadn't even realized he was missing the family thing, but having Mallie there, with the two kids, just made everything feel so much different.

The fact that she was smiling, and that they were all helping, made something that could have been a major pain in the butt or, at the very least, something that ruined their day into something that they actually enjoyed.

It was also something that made him realize that Mallie was probably different than most of the other women that he knew. And maybe it wasn't just Mallie who had had the Lord open the door for her to walk through.

It wasn't that the day had been perfect. Far from it. It was hot. Sweat trickled down his temples and down the small of his back. His armpits felt wet. He had been clean, but he had dust on his jeans from kneeling in the dirt, and his hands were filthy as well.

There were bugs and flies, and he was thirsty.

But despite all those things that he knew were wrong, it was easier to focus on the positive when the person he was with was smiling and happy and didn't seem the slightest bit bothered by any of the things that were annoying him.

He supposed that the idea of spending time with someone who made him better was part of what he was thinking as well.

Or maybe it was that he didn't want to be the weak link. The one who complained. Regardless of what it was, when he spent time with someone who made him focus on the good rather than the bad, it was always a blessing. That would be the kind of person he wanted to be married to.

# Chapter 13

They arrived at the ranch later than expected due to the flat tire. Mallie wasn't sure exactly what she had been expecting, but it wasn't the obvious money and luxury that met her as they drove under the arched gate and down the fence-lined drive.

"My sister envisioned horses in these fields. She loved horses."

"Florence's mom?" Mallie asked, just wanting to make sure. He said Florence was his niece, but he hadn't talked much about his sister.

"Yeah."

"I want to ride horses!" Evangeline said from the back.

"Me too," Eli echoed.

"Not today. We don't have horses yet, but maybe someday."

Mallie heard him, but she wasn't really paying attention. His truck wasn't a newer model, and the air-conditioning had been broken, then the flat tire. She hadn't exactly thought he was destitute, but she assumed that he was solidly middle-class or slightly below.

She hadn't really been concerned about his money or his financial situation. That hadn't mattered, other than making sure that the bills were paid and that he was the kind of man who paid his bills on time.

But this... "Is this yours?" She nodded at the low, sprawling ranch house that came into view. There was an A-frame front with huge windows covering the entire front side, and two sides that came out like wings.

It was the biggest house she'd ever seen, in North Dakota anyway.

"It is. Don't you like it?" His tone held concern, like he actually thought she was unhappy with what she saw.

"I guess. I'm just surprised."

She didn't know what else to say. Fresh mulch lined the white cement sidewalk, and bushes that looked like they'd been freshly planted in a manicured and well-kept bed sat snug up against the front of the two wings.

The gravel drive they had been on became concrete as they slipped into the circle that curved around the front of the house.

The middle of the circle had a fountain, with water shooting up in the air.

"Cool! You have a water fountain!" Eli exclaimed.

"You have a water fountain," Mallie echoed, looking over at Jones, her brows lifted. He was living in a duplex, drove a truck where the air conditioner was broken, and she had not been expecting this excessive display of money as they pulled up to the ranch he claimed was his.

"I guess we have to talk about a few things. I... I have some things to tell you."

She almost rolled her eyes, thinking, *A few*? But she didn't say anything. She wasn't angry, just surprised. A little flabbergasted maybe. He hadn't seemed like the type to live in such splendor.

"You guys want to see the water fountain?" he asked, looking in the rearview mirror at the twins who nodded their heads eagerly.

They pulled to a stop, and Mallie got out without saying anything more. She didn't know what else to say.

They took the kids' hands, and they must have spent a full ten minutes walking around the water fountain, watching the water squirt up in the air.

Mallie had to admit, the sound of the water was soothing and she enjoyed watching it too. There was just something about water that was calming and beautiful.

"All right, guys, let's go around back. I'm pretty sure there's a swing set back there." The kids squealed and hurried around the house while Mallie tried to control her terror. She hadn't realized that Jones was...rich.

She wasn't sure exactly why that scared her, but she knew he was way out of her depth. She'd never had much at all, and even less after her divorce. She was living in a duplex, for goodness' sake.

Not that there was anything wrong with that, it was just a far cry from this massive mansion in front of her that had a fountain, a cement driveway, and a really large swing set that would rival any swing set in any park she'd ever been to.

"So maybe you can tell me who you are?" she asked as the kids ran to the swing set, and Eli immediately started climbing to the very highest point he could, while Evangeline sat more sedately on a swing and started trying to push herself, more or less successfully.

"My sister was Annika. Country music superstar."

Mallie took a few moments to digest that information. Annika. Who didn't recognize that name? It was maybe not quite as big as Elvis, but she was definitely the kind of superstar who was known by her first name only.

But she had been killed in an airplane crash about a year ago or so, if Mallie remembered correctly.

"So you are raising Florence, Annika's daughter?"

"Yes."

"Since she passed away?" She shuddered, thinking of the terrible tragedy Annika's death had been.

"Yeah. Florence's father died in a car accident before she was born. I... I always sang backup for Annika, we toured together, and I was always there. I...was not exactly a father to her, but sometimes it felt that way."

"You two obviously have a strong bond. I noticed that when we were singing together, just from observing you. She seems very comfortable with you and obviously loves you. You love her as well."

"I do. She's like a daughter to me. I don't have any children, so I guess I don't really know what that feels like, but I can't imagine loving a child more than I love Florence."

She knew that to be true. Just from observing him.

"So that explains why everything is so...over-the-top rich." She sighed, looking at the swing set but not really seeing it. She had not expected this wrinkle.

Of course, it was kind of ironic that she would go from worrying about how she was going to pay the bills to worrying about how she was going to be so rich.

"And you really want to marry...me?" she asked, letting the tone of her voice convey how ludicrous that idea was.

"I told you, it was Florence's idea. But I have to say, the more time I spend with you, the more I think her idea is a very good one."

Mallie shrugged her shoulders and shook her head. She would have to think about that for a while. She couldn't imagine that someone who could have anyone would pop the question to someone he didn't even know. Someone like her.

"And I wasn't kidding. She really does need a nanny, someone to keep an eye on her over the summer as I'll be coming and going. She's obviously old enough to take care of herself, but I can't just leave her alone. It'd be nice if you do some cooking, although I'll have a housecleaner and someone to take care of the yard work."

"I don't mind cooking or cleaning, although if I were to be living here, I would expect the girls to do their share of cooking and cleaning as well."

"I think that's good for them."

He met her eyes, and she thought she saw that he agreed with her philosophy that kids should help around the house. Even if they didn't have to or could afford to hire someone to do the work for them.

"So that explains why you sing and play the guitar."

"I wrote a lot of Annika's songs. I sang with her. She actually wanted us to be a duo, but I didn't want the spotlight."

"I understand that."

"But I might not have a choice. My agent is after me to write and record, and while the money that we have from what Annika has done is sufficient, I have to admit I love music. And there definitely is a pull to get back in."

"There are probably people who are depending on you as well."

"There's that too."

"Is there a recording studio in the house?" That might explain part of the reason why it was so big.

"There is. In the basement, to try to keep the outside noise down. I'll show it to you if you want to see it."

"It's okay. I was just wondering. If you can do a lot of your recording here, then that might cut down the amount of time that you have to travel. That would be good for Florence."

"That's exactly what Annika was thinking. She loved North Dakota, having visited a couple of times, and she wanted to be able to do as much of her work here as she could. She loved the idea of being snowed in over the winter." He laughed a little at that, and Mallie had to shake her head.

"There's something to be said for being snowed in. Although, I prefer to be snowed in with electricity. It gets a little chilly if you don't have a way to heat your house."

"I bet."

Silence fell between them as they watched the kids climbing on the monkey bars. They were laughing, and the sound drifted toward them on the breeze. The sun shone down, and Mallie had to admit she was getting a little warmer than was comfortable.

As though Jones could read her mind, he said, "Do you want to go over to the shade and sit down on the bench?"

"Sure," she said, falling into stride beside him as they walked over and sat down.

The kids called for them to watch, and they waved and talked to them a little bit, until the children's attention was caught on something else and they forgot about the adults.

"Does this change your mind about wanting to get married?"

"No. I guess not. I was going to ask for a bit of a background check or some references or something, but I think I'll be able to Google you now and see if you've ever been arrested at least."

"If I had, I'm sure that would end up on the news and you would be able to find that pretty easily online."

"That's exactly what I was thinking." She sighed. She couldn't remember ever hearing anything bad about him in the news, but she didn't exactly follow the lifestyle and every move of any celebrity, and definitely not country music stars. "I thought you might want some references from me."

"I can ask around town about you. I grew up in a small town, and I know how they are. Everybody will know you, and I'll get a pretty good idea of who you are."

"I'm sure you're right." She wasn't afraid. There were probably some people in town who didn't care for her, for one reason or another, although she hadn't heard of anyone, and to her knowledge, there wasn't anyone that she didn't get along with. But some people could find a way to criticize anyone. For anything.

And it might be good if Jones figured out all of her bad qualities and decided to marry her anyway. That way he wouldn't be surprised when they got together.

"Is there anything else you can think of that you want to ask me?"

"Not really, other than I suppose it would be nice to know how much time you think you're going to be spending away and how much time you expect to be home. Not that I want you to be gone, but just...to give me an idea of what I'm getting myself into. I don't think taking care of two girls is going to be that much more difficult than taking care of one. It might actually be easier in some ways because Toni will have a built-in playmate, as will Florence."

"As long as they don't start fighting. That could drive you insane. I remember my sister and I fought terribly from about eighth grade to tenth grade, and then we ended up being best friends. But that was about the time we started singing together too."

"Yeah. I guess with one child, you don't have to worry about fighting with anyone else."

"My mom always said it was the bickering that always got to her, but maybe they're at the age where they'll just get along."

"That sounds a little bit like wishful thinking, but I suppose it could be true."

They sat there for a bit longer before the kids came over saying that they were thirsty.

Jones took them in the kitchen door, the side door which led directly to the huge chef's kitchen.

Mallie had to try to remember to keep her mouth closed and not gawk like she'd never been in such an amazing kitchen before. Although she hadn't.

After the kids had a drink, he led them around the living room and the den and the sunroom, which Mallie loved and was already outfitted with plants.

Workers were doing some trim work and seemed to be installing the last of the flooring and hardware such as lights and doorknobs.

"It's going a lot faster than what I thought, and it's going to be ready to move in next week."

"All right."

"I was thinking that we would get married...Tuesday?"

She tried not to swallow her tongue. That would be awkward, so she cleared her throat and said, "Tuesday?"

"Is that too soon for you?"

"No. It's not. I think if we're going to do it, we might as well do it, right?"

She wanted to talk to him about what exactly they were going to expect out of the marriage, but as he led them around, the twins seemed to get more and more tired, until finally she was carrying Evangeline and he was carrying Eli, and they were both saying they were hungry, with Evangeline sticking her thumb in her mouth.

"I know there's a couple ready-made meals in the refrigerator. I ordered a few for Florence and I in case we spent whole days out here, as we did on Saturday. If you don't mind, we'll head in there to eat, and then it looks like these two are ready for a nap."

"Yes. I wasn't sure whether we should put them down here or go home. I like to be home when Toni gets off the bus. If I'm not going to be there, I usually try to let her know. Although I could text her if you think it's better to stay."

"It's liable to get loud here, and the noises they're not used to might wake them up. Let's go home, but I definitely want to have an appointment with you for tomorrow. Unless you think that it would be better to wait."

"No. Like I just said, if we're going to do it, we might as well do it."

She just hoped that she wasn't being foolish, but she thought that it might be silly to overthink it. She just needed to do it. Put one foot in front of the other and just move. If it turned out to be a mistake, it wouldn't be the first mistake she'd ever made in her life, and it wouldn't be one she couldn't correct.

"I suppose you'll want to get a prenup drawn up. Is there enough time for that?"

He paused in the act of opening the refrigerator and turned around and looked at her. "I hadn't considered a prenup, but I don't like the idea. That's almost like saying, we know we're not going to stay together, so here's how we're going to split. And... I know I have the most to lose, but I'd rather take a chance on you. I expect this to be forever. And I'm hoping you do too."

"I do, but I want you to be protected. I don't want people to say that I was some kind of gold digger, trying to grab you because of your money."

"I've definitely had people who've tried to do that, and I understand what you're saying, but no. No prenup." He tilted his head, hesitated as though he were considering his next words carefully, then said, "I'd love for us to sing together—in public—as a family."

# Chapter 14

"**Y**ou don't look happy," Jones said, leaning forward and trying to meet her gaze.

She bent her head. She needed to be straight with him. Taking a breath and plunging in, she said, "I've never wanted to be famous. I've never wanted to be rich. I've never even thought about it. But the idea of trading my time and my privacy in order to have money, in order to be popular, in order to sell my product... I just don't want to do that. At least, it's scary."

Maybe it wasn't everything she wanted to say, but it was a start. She'd seen so many celebrities who seemed to crash and burn when fame and fortune got too big for them to handle. Their marriages didn't work out, their family split apart, nothing seemed to go right, and they seemed to need more and more attention, never satisfied with what they had, and always trying to do more, have more, be more. Enough was just never enough.

She couldn't remember ever hearing about issues like that with Annika or hearing any problems that her band members might have had. But again, she didn't typically follow celebrity news.

"I'll be honest and say that's my least favorite part of my job. I don't like walking down the street and having people recognize me. That really wasn't something that I typically had a problem with, but I would be with Annika, and people would stop her in the street. They'd think I was her husband, and they'd want to take our pictures and want her autograph, and they'd want to talk to her like they were best friends, and I did not love it, but I can see how it can be addicting."

Mallie nodded right away. That was exactly what she had meant. That fame was addicting, that people did things just to get their name in the paper. That they needed that affirmation, because they couldn't find their worth in the Lord, and so they tried to find it in their friends and money and fame, and somehow the adulation of all their fans wasn't enough.

"I don't know that I want to draw my daughter into that either."

"Annika worked hard to keep Flo out of the spotlight. She wouldn't allow her to be photographed, and she insisted on her privacy. She went to great lengths for it. That might be part of the reason why she chose North Dakota."

It was true that all the country music superstars seemed to make their home in Tennessee. Annika couldn't have been more different in choosing North Dakota.

"It sounds to me like she wanted the best for Florence, but weren't there long stretches where Florence didn't see her?"

"Yes, there were. And that's unavoidable. She had times where she couldn't make it home between shows, or she had to practice, or different things. She did her best."

"I believe she did. I'm sure she was a great mom. Flo seems like a well-rounded child, although I'm sure that a lot of that credit goes to you, too." He did seem like a great dad/uncle. Whatever he considered himself. It was obvious that Florence loved him. "Still, that's a big difference in lifestyle between what Toni and I are used to. I... I'm not saying I won't do it, but I just have a lot of reservations."

"That's understandable. Maybe we need to work through those before we see the preacher. Because that's going to be my life. I don't particularly like the spotlight, and I don't necessarily need a ton of money, but I was fine with Annika keeping her money, and I invested mine back in the business. That's where my investments are." He shook his head. "I didn't realize she was going to die. But I invested in a lot of equipment. While she built the house, I took care of the music. I always paid the best band members we could find, I did a lot of advertising, before we hired an agency, just put a lot of what I earned back into the business."

"I see. And it seems like it would have been a solid investment."

"It should have been. She had the kind of career that would span a lifetime. But..."

He looked down; it was obvious that he still missed his sister. His mouth was tight, and his eyes sad.

Mallie didn't know what to say. She had never lost a sibling, and she figured that had to hurt. To leave a hole, someone who could share childhood memories, someone to laugh with and talk about your parents with.

Of course, her daughter didn't have siblings either. And she'd always wanted her to. She wanted a big family after growing up as an only child. It would have been nice to have playmates.

"How about you think about it? I can't make any promises to quit, because I'm committed. I've already taken a year off, and that was more than anyone wanted me to. But I had to make sure that Florence was grounded."

"I get it. How soon do you think you need to leave?"

"I have a meeting scheduled for later this week in Tennessee. I was really hoping that I would have someone to watch Florence by the time I had to leave."

"Then I guess we can go ahead with the marriage as scheduled. When I agreed, I gave my word. And I suppose even though there are going to be things that I don't like, I'm sure you're going to put up with things that you don't like either. That just seems to be the way marriages go, right?"

"That's right. I appreciate your commitment."

She was glad he could see that. Although that wasn't what she had intended when she spoke. But she supposed it was true. A marriage couldn't last if one of the people in it wasn't committed.

# Chapter 15

Travis held the paper in his hand, staring at the words.

Ellen's handwriting. He traced a finger over it and then looked out the window of his studio apartment.

It was small, and he had to pay for it. Ford was giving him the chance of a lifetime, but he wasn't just handing everything over. Travis didn't mind. He knew that in order to be a success in life, a person couldn't have things handed to them. They had to work for them. And he didn't mind the hard work.

He did mind that Ellen thought that he had gone to see Shanna while he was home.

He had heard from Mr. Tadgh that one of his brothers was having trouble in school. He told Ford that he needed to take a quick trip home, and then he drove all night so that he could wake his brother Roger up first thing in the morning and have a long talk.

Roger hadn't been too receptive at first, and Travis wasn't sure he ever did get through to him, but he had done his best. That was the second hard thing about being gone—he wasn't there to babysit his brothers, and they needed to be self-motivated. Roger needed to set the example for his little brother.

He thought he'd gotten through to him, but he wasn't sure. After all, none of them wanted to end up like their mother who wasn't even home the morning he'd gotten there.

When Roger had asked him what he was doing, he hadn't wanted to tell him that he was driving straight back to Chicago and digging into work. He wasn't sure why, maybe he didn't want Roger to know that he drove all night just to talk to him. Maybe he didn't want Roger to know that all he did was work and eat and sleep, and he didn't always do a lot of eating, since he had to cook everything himself. But most likely, he didn't want Roger to know how much he longed to see Ellen.

And how much he knew he shouldn't. After all, she was still so much younger than he was, still under the age of consent, and he could be in big trouble if he got caught doing any of the things that he wanted to do. Things he knew he shouldn't be doing anyway, so there was that, too.

Ellen deserved a man who would respect her and would wait for her. That's what he wanted to be. The man who respected and waited for her.

So, he just casually mentioned a party so that his brothers wouldn't grill him about it anymore. And then, once they got on the bus, he got back in his car and went to see his mom. That had been a waste of time, since she'd been hungover at the apartment where Roger had said he thought her newest boyfriend lived.

She hadn't been happy to see him, even though it had been several months since she'd seen him last. And he'd given up and driven home. To Chicago. Which was not home.

He kinda felt that wherever Ellen was was home.

But his brothers had big mouths, and they'd told Ellen he'd gone to see Shanna, and of course Ellen knew he hadn't taken the time to see Ellen.

She was hurt, and rightfully so. After all, he was much better friends with Ellen than he was with Shanna, whom he only knew on a casual, very casual, basis.

She only wanted to use him, while Ellen had truly cared.

Maybe Shanna cared in her own way. And maybe Shanna was a really nice person, but she wasn't the kind of person that he wanted to get to know. That was Ellen.

Now what?

He wanted to set the lie straight, but he realized this for the gift it was. If Ellen didn't care for him at all, he wouldn't have any trouble staying away. She wouldn't let him close.

Although Ellen was such a softhearted person, she'd probably forgive him immediately and welcome him back.

He pressed his lips together and looked out the window.

He wanted to go home. Home where he could look off into the distance and see nothing but waving grass and wide blue sky, puffy clouds, and feel the wind on his face, and smell the wildness.

But he had to put his time in here first. He told Ford he would. He had to keep his word. Plus, there was no point going home, except to take care of his brothers. Ellen wasn't nearly ready, and he needed to stay away.

*Lord, I need to be just friends with Ellen. I need to be a friend to her. She needs a friend.*

He hadn't been a very good friend. She'd been far better to him than he had been to her.

And now this.

What was he going to say to her? How could he explain that in a way that she would believe?

He wanted her to know that he cared for her, but he had to be careful. His feelings had to stay friend only.

Could he do that?

He sat down at his small kitchen table and started to write.

*Dear Ellen,*

*You're right. Shanna isn't a friend. Not really. She's been nice to me, in her own way, and I talked to her some, spent a little time with her. But you've been a true friend.*

*I hurt you. And I'm sorry.*

He chewed on the end of his pencil. He kept a whole pack of pencils and a sharpener, just for Ellen. She'd wanted to write letters, and he'd wanted to do whatever she wanted. Funny, the things a man would do for the woman he loved.

Although, Ellen was only fourteen. She was hardly a woman.

Although she was definitely mature for her age. Being an only child caused her to grow up more quickly, and maybe being raised by her uncle had helped with that as well.

She'd also helped on the farm and been a part of making his Highland cow business a success.

She seemed more mature than even girls his age.

Regardless. Could he explain to her what he had done?

*I've never lied to you, and I hope I never start.*

*I didn't see Shanna. I told the boys I might be going to a party later, because I didn't want them to know that I was going to say something to our mom, who was hungover at her boyfriend's apartment, and also I didn't want them pressuring me to go see you.*

*I know, you don't understand why I didn't want to see you, and trust me, it's not because I truly didn't want to see you. It was just because I know it's not a good idea.*

*It makes me want things that I can't have. I want to move back home to North Dakota. I want out of the city. I hate it here. Although, I try to see the good, but there isn't much. It stinks, it's crowded, and nobody cares.*

*It's nothing like North Dakota, nothing like Sweet Water.*

*Anyway, I'm here, and I'm going to stay, and I need to make it so that I don't want a bunch of things I can't have. I hope you understand. I'm sorry.*

*Thank you for telling me about your dog. She sounds sweet. I'm sure you're patient with her. I've heard they're hard to train but very intelligent and loyal. Just the kind of dog that I would think someone like you would have. And I mean that in a good way. Because it would take a lot of patience, and you always had a lot of patience with me.*

He thought about the things he'd been learning with Mr. Hansen, and he wrote some of them down, not a lot. Mr. Hansen did a lot of things that he didn't like to talk to people about. It wasn't that he was secretive, just that he kept things close to the vest. And for good reason, the business was cutthroat, and people would steal ideas if they could and pass them off as their own.

Mr. Hansen had emphasized how important it was to be honest, but at the same time, he also said that while it's good to help people, it's also good to not get too mouthy about what you're doing.

So he just said,

> *I am learning a lot of good things. Things that I think will help me when I start my own business. I haven't quite decided what that's going to be yet. I know that sounds crazy. I just know I want to build something.*

He wanted to do it with Ellen beside him, but he wasn't going to put that in the letter. Not yet. Maybe not ever. After all, he knew that if he insisted on just being friends, Ellen might find someone else.

If that happened, he wasn't sure he'd ever get married, but he assumed that God would know. He'd have to believe that she would be there for him, if he did what he knew was right now.

> *I miss you all. I miss hearing about your cows, I hope Daisy's okay. I know you said you were going to breed her last fall so she'd have a spring calf. I guess you are looking forward to that. Maybe you can send me pictures; does anyone print pictures anymore?*
>
> *Well, regardless, if you can't send me a picture, you have to describe her to me. In the meantime, I better go. I bought some macaroni and cheese, and I'm going to try to make it. Up until this point, I've just been cooking pizza in the oven and eating the leftovers for the rest of the week.*

*You be good, and thanks for looking after my brothers.*
*Your friend,*
*Travis*

# Chapter 16

*Lord, I pray that You heal my marriage. Please give me the patience that it takes to be kind to my husband. Help me to be forgiving. Help me not to hold things against him. Help me not to try to hurt him the way he's hurt me. Help me to return kindness for the evil that he's done to me, and help me to remember that You love him, and You want me to love him too. Amen.*

June stayed on her knees beside her bed, her hands clasped. Even though she said amen, she continued to pray, continue to plead for her marriage; she didn't want to be divorced. Even though her children had said it was okay, even though her counselor had said she couldn't believe that she had put up with her husband for so long, she wanted there to be a happy ending for her. She wanted to keep her vows. She didn't want to be divorced.

She never thought she would end up divorced.

Still, she had made an effort to see what it would take to leave.

To get a divorce without hiring a lawyer to figure that much out. She also had almost enough money saved up to buy a home. One that wouldn't require a lot of upkeep on her part, since she was a woman alone and wouldn't be able to do a whole lot of yard work or that type of thing. Although, she'd always wanted to garden. She even looked at a couple of houses.

But she hadn't given up on her marriage.

Her brows drew down when she heard what sounded like her husband's pickup pulling into the drive.

Usually he wasn't home at this time during the day.

She took a breath. She had a couple of ideas that she wanted to run by him, hoping that he would agree to at least one. Hoping that there would be a solution to their marriage issues, and she wouldn't have to continue to move toward divorce.

Looking in the mirror, surprised at the old lady that looked back at her, she smoothed her hair down and tried to smile.

It was always a shock when she looked like she was her age, rather than like she was a teenager or maybe in her twenties.

Where had the time gone?

She'd raised a whole family and had all of her children out in the world.

This was supposed to be the time where she and her husband enjoyed their empty nest, enjoyed fairly good health, and learned to love each other again.

Instead of her thinking that she was going to leave.

Walking down the stairs, she met her husband as he walked in the front door from work.

"Hello, Wayne."

"June. I thought you'd be napping."

She pressed her lips together. He never thought she did anything. In fact, she'd worked for eight hours already, on her online business, and had knelt to pray before she got up to come down and cook herself a midafternoon snack.

"No. I'm not napping."

He grunted.

"Wayne?"

He grunted again.

"I was thinking it would be fun if we took a trip to Hawaii."

He snorted. And turned to her. "You're serious?"

"Yeah. Hawaii is romantic. And I just thought it would be nice for you and I to get away together."

She hadn't finished talking before his lips pressed together and he started shaking his head.

"If you want to go to Hawaii, you can go ahead and go. But I don't have time for that kind of foolishness. Nor do I want to waste money like that."

She kind of figured that was going to be his answer, but she swallowed her disappointment anyway. Somehow, she always believed that this time was going to be different. This time he was going to want to be with her. He was going to say *oh yes, I was hoping we could spend more time together, because you're such a fun person. I love being with you. I love the way I feel when I'm with you. Love the way we laugh together, and I'd love to get to know you even better.* Something foolish along those lines.

She had been a very young woman when she'd given up those dreams.

"All right."

He started to walk away.

"Wayne?"

"Now what?"

"Would you go to marriage counseling with me?" She couldn't really get that out of her mouth in a confident way. She'd asked multiple times over the course of their marriage if he would go, and his reply had always been, "I don't think there's anything wrong with our marriage. But you go if you want to. I wouldn't mind having a better wife. It'd be nice if you were more like my dog. Maybe a marriage counselor can help you with that."

He shook his head and rolled his eyes. "Why are you always asking me stupid stuff like that?" His voice held disgust. "What's a marriage counselor gonna say? I mean, you could use some help, but she can't change perfection." He stuck his chest out. "Now, I forgot some papers I need, and I'm going to go get them, and I need to get back to work. I didn't mean to wake you up from your nap."

She didn't say anything as he walked out of the room.

She swallowed hard again, feeling her eyes tighten, like she wanted to cry, but she tried as hard as she could to keep from letting the tears flow.

She didn't want to cry over him anymore. She'd already shed so many tears. When she'd been alone, when he told her yet again that he didn't want her or want to spend time with her, when he'd forgotten her anniversary, or her birthday, and had told her that he had no idea what to get her for Christmas, so he didn't get her anything.

Gifts really didn't matter, but it was the idea that he hadn't thought of her at all.

Not even a little. Not even enough to get her a candy bar. Or a vase of flowers, which wouldn't have been her favorite thing, but at least it would have shown that he was thinking of her.

She wasn't the slightest bit hungry, but she didn't want to slink away until after he had left, so she got a carrot out and set it on the counter, then grabbed an onion and started to chop it into small pieces.

She could pretend for a little longer.

It wasn't five minutes later that he walked back through the kitchen, waving the papers.

"Don't hold supper, I'll be late," he said as he walked out. Not waiting for her to answer before he shut the door.

Right. At least he told her; usually he didn't. Typically she had no idea what time he was going to come home.

And that seemed to be just fine with him.

# Chapter 17

Noise caused Helen to look up from her quilting where she'd been immersed for the last several hours.

Her hand went to her throat when she realized it was the sound of her husband's pickup truck coming into the lane.

She glanced at the clock to confirm her suspicions as her heart skipped a beat.

She had been so engrossed in her quilting that she had totally forgotten about supper.

Shutting off the audiobook that played in the background, she scrambled to her feet as fast as her age would allow her to.

Maybe faster. Because her back seized up, and she threw a hand behind her, rubbing the offending spot as she continued to straighten with a little bit more dignity.

Because of her back, she hadn't quite made it to the middle of the room when the door opened and Edgar walked in.

"Hello," she said, trying not to squeak.

"Hey there," he said, with a little bit of a smile. Ever since she'd taken to greeting him at the door, he started to act like he expected to see her and...was happy to.

"I have a small confession to make," she said, knowing that he wouldn't be angry, just knowing that she considered making supper her job, and she didn't like to drop the ball. It would be like him oversleeping and not making it to work on time. She wouldn't appreciate him taking his employment so lightly, and she couldn't expect him to be okay with her forgetting to do one of the things he depended on her for.

"Okay?" he said slowly but still with a bit of a smile, like he was confident that whatever she was going to confess wasn't going to be that bad.

"I have supper partially started, but the time got away from me, and it's not ready yet." She scrunched up her brows and finished moving toward him, wrapping her arms around him. "I'm sorry."

She hadn't hugged him when he got home from work for years, possibly a decade or more. She didn't know when they'd dropped that habit. It used to be that she and the kids would eagerly wait at the door, and they would greet him with affection, a hug and a kiss and something cold to drink.

The years had gone by, and she had to force herself to get into the habit of even acknowledging that he made it home.

"That's fine. What are you planning on having? I can give you a hand with it."

She couldn't help herself, she froze. "Really?"

"Sure. Back in the day, I used to cook more than a little. Remember? I used to cook Sunday breakfast all the time."

"That's right. You did. You said that was my day to sleep in after being up every night with the baby."

"That's how it started, but even when the kids were in elementary school, I enjoyed getting up and making breakfast with them on Sunday mornings."

"And I enjoyed getting up to the smell of bacon and coffee, with no work required on my part."

"I can't believe the kids are grown and out of the house."

"Me either," she said, and they stepped back away from each other, but he kept his arm around her. She liked that. Especially since they looked into each other's eyes and talked about memories and things they had done together.

"All right. You tell me what to do, and we can get started. I'm hungry."

"I'm hungry too."

"Is that what kept you from my food?" he asked, nodding at the dining room table where all of her quilting things were spread out.

"Yeah. I was listening to a really great book, and time just seemed to fly as I put the pattern together, and... I don't know. I just had a really nice afternoon."

"I'm glad. That looks pretty."

Pink was not his favorite color, and there was a good bit of pink and purple in the quilt, but she appreciated his compliment anyway. "Thank you."

"Are you giving that to someone?" he asked, and again it struck her that he knew that she usually made quilts and gave them to friends or to people who needed them. Sometimes she donated them to charity auctions, and sometimes she mailed them clear across the country. It just depended on what need came up.

"I haven't decided who's getting it yet. I guess the need just hasn't come across my radar yet."

He had never complained about the amount of money she spent on material to feed her quilting addiction.

Of course, she was doing good in the world, and he was getting credit because he paid for the material while she put in the work. But still... "Thank you for never complaining about the money I spend on my quilting supplies."

"It makes me feel good that you help other people and spend your time in a constructive way. I guess I wouldn't care if I came home and you were watching TV, but I suppose I would feel a little less indulgent if I had to pay for that."

She knew he didn't mean it in an authoritarian kind of way. She understood what he was saying. That he didn't mind the expense because it was something she loved and was also a worthwhile thing.

"I was going to make walking tacos, and I have hamburger in the skillet, I just need to cook it. I also need these vegetables chopped up," she said, indicating the onion and the lettuce that she pulled out of the refrigerator and set on the counter next to the cutting board.

"I can do it," he said, reaching for a knife and grabbing the onion.

It was on the tip of her tongue to tell him that the knife he had picked up was a steak knife and not supposed to be used for cutting onions.

Did it matter?

She also wanted to tell him to wash his hands first. But she didn't. Were there really going to be germs on his hands that would kill them?

Most likely not, and he was doing something kind for her. For the first time in a long time, they were going to cook together, and she didn't want to ruin it by criticizing every move he made.

So, despite the fact that she knew that he would do better with a different knife, and she would prefer that he wash his hands, she pursed her lips closed and determined that she wasn't going to try to micromanage everything he did. She would just appreciate what he gave her.

A part of her brain said that asking someone to wash their hands wasn't nitpicking, but another part said that it really didn't matter in the long run. Ten years from now, was it going to matter if he washed his hands?

It would not. So, she concentrated on enjoying the fact that he was in the kitchen with her and tried not to worry about whatever he was doing that she thought should be done a different way.

There were no rules that said her way was the right way, even if it was her kitchen.

After they had chatted about his day at work just a little, he said, "You know, you used to be a lot more critical."

"What do you mean?" she asked, pushing the hamburger around the skillet so that it browned evenly.

"I just mean that anytime I was in the kitchen with you, it always had to be done your way, or you told me how I wasn't doing it right, and I didn't really enjoy working with you very much."

Ouch. That hurt.

She swallowed, determined not to get offended. After all, he was just telling her the truth. "I can see why. I don't really enjoy working with people who constantly criticize everything I do, either. I guess... I guess I was just young and dumb."

"And now you're wise and...not quite as young."

She laughed at the way he stumbled a little, because he was going to call her old. "It's okay. I'm old. And you can say it."

"You're not supposed to give a woman a hard time about being...not young anymore."

They laughed again, because he still refused to say the O word.

"I'm being serious. I've forgotten how much I enjoy being with you. Maybe I didn't enjoy cooking with you, but...we used to have fun together." He sounded a little sad and melancholy.

"So... We don't have to make that all past tense, do we? I mean, we can still have fun together? I like being with you. I guess it's mostly my fault. I'm the one who slacked off. I just thought today how I used to meet you with a hug and a cold drink, and I don't do that anymore."

"I always looked forward to coming home. Some guys complained about their families, complained about their wives, made it seem like they'd almost rather be at work than at home. Or they'd go to a bar after work, because they didn't really want to go home. But I always looked forward to it. You made our home a happy place."

His words made her chest swell with happiness. She had tried. She had tried hard to make their home a place where people smiled and laughed and joked and felt comfortable. Where their kids loved to bring their friends, and everyone enjoyed hanging out. It was a home where the people in it were more important than things. But she'd lost that as the children left and she got more involved in the work that she did and in hobbies for herself. Her husband had been neglected.

In return, he had neglected her. But she hadn't seen anything but his neglect.

"Thank you. I did try hard. But I guess I slacked off," she said. She reached for the taco seasoning and shook it on the hamburger that was almost finished cooking.

"I suppose it's never too late to turn over a new leaf. After all, I'm just as not young as you are."

She smiled at his continued avoidance and shook her head. "I've never agreed with that saying where you can't teach an old dog new tricks. I feel like you can."

"Maybe you can teach a pair of old dogs new tricks if they're determined to learn them together."

"You know, you always made me laugh. Always. And that made things so much easier." She set the spice back in the cupboard and closed the door. "I'm definitely down for learning some new tricks."

"That's great. Because I was thinking we should buy a set of motorcycles and travel the country."

Helen jerked around, her eyeballs about popping out of her head. "A motorcycle?" Did he really think that she was the kind of person who could drive a motorcycle?

"Sure. I see people on them all the time. In fact, just yesterday at the drive-through I saw a lady in a skirt riding a moped. Why not?"

Indeed. Why not?

"You said you always wanted to go see Yellowstone. Something about those big trees out there, and some kind of hot water thing. Let's do it. Let's get mopeds, then pack our stuff and go take a trip. I've got a ton of vacation saved up, and we could take three months and just go see the country."

She did not want to do that. She did not want to drive a two-wheeled anything. Not even a bicycle. She was...not young.

But she could see the light in her husband's eyes, see it was something he was offering as a peace offering, since she loved to travel and he didn't.

Although why couldn't they do it in a car like normal people?

*You wanted to be closer to your husband. He just asked you to take a three-month trip with him, and he looks excited about it. Are you really going to turn him down?*

"Okay," she said, and she made her lips turn up into a smile. She was not going to be one of those people who had to have their way all the time and couldn't enjoy something if it wasn't their idea. It was just three months of her life, and then they would be home, and she would have the memories. Why not make them good ones?

"You don't sound very excited," he said, putting the onion aside and starting to chop up the lettuce.

"I'm talking myself into it. I think it's going to be fun. I think the memories are going to be great. And... I love that you want to do that with me. And you're right, I do want to see the redwoods and Old Faithful, the geyser you were talking about. And I want to go to the top of the Rockies and see the view. See the ocean and watch the sunset. There's tons of things I'd love to do. I think there's a whole road along the Pacific Ocean from Oregon down to the southern part of California. That would be a fun ride."

"We can get a map and start planning our route. We can get it figured out down to where we'd stay. I know you love those kinds of things. To have it all planned out."

"I know. You're more spur of the moment. We don't have to have every single thing figured out. Maybe we can just take roads that look interesting."

"You don't want to go east? To New England? Or Florida?"

"The Florida Keys would be fun. And I guess I've never really been anywhere out east. So I'm game for anything."

"You are starting to get excited about it now."

"As long as you're there, I think we'll have fun. Let's do it!"

# Chapter 18

It took a little longer than what they thought, but it worked out perfectly that the last day of school had been the day before, and their wedding was the first day of summer vacation.

They also had been cleared to move into the ranch house, which was not quite finished, but the odds and ends that needed to be done would not keep them from being able to live in it.

Mallie tried not to fidget as Toni walked beside her, her arm around her waist, beaming.

Toni had wanted a father for so long, and she begged and begged for Mallie to find someone.

Interestingly, Mallie hadn't been super interested, and while she had been willing to take whoever the Lord had sent, she also didn't really think God was going to send anyone, so when she told Toni that they just needed to leave it in the Lord's hands, she figured she'd be single for the rest of her life.

But today was her wedding day.

Her second wedding day.

Would this marriage turn out differently than her first?

She was almost positive it would. First of all, she was older, wiser, hopefully not as prone to making the same stupid mistakes.

She could see, from the wisdom that came with age, she supposed, that the destruction of her first marriage had not been entirely her ex's fault.

Although at the time it felt like it was all him, she could see that she could have been a better wife, a better person. More patient, less critical, more understanding when he wasn't perfect.

Of course, that might not have been what drove him to cheat, and even if it had been, he should have had the character to not run off with someone else. So there was definitely nothing she could do there. She certainly couldn't help someone develop character when he was determined to not. But she hadn't been perfect, and she felt like she needed to admit that.

"Are you okay?" Jones asked from beside her.

She gave him a smile that felt tremulous. "I'm fine."

"Just fine?" His brows raised, as though he was willing to not do it if she wasn't a lot better than fine.

"I'm nervous. I was thinking that this is my second wedding day and my first marriage wasn't exactly a roaring success. I did get Toni, and she's been worth everything..." She laughed. "I didn't think about it, but I'm getting another daughter with this marriage, and I'm definitely excited about that." She looked over at Florence, who smiled at her words.

Mallie wasn't under any illusions that Florence was ready to have another mother. She might not ever be ready for that. Mothers held a special place in a person's heart, and that place couldn't usually be taken by someone else. But maybe there would be room for two.

"I'm nervous too. I'm glad I'm not alone. What started out as a crazy idea kinda feels right to me."

Hearing Jones say those words made her straighten her shoulders and pick up her chin. "It feels right to me too. I guess I was just wallowing in the past a little. Wondering if I've learned anything since the last time I did this. Because while it's always nice to blame other people, I need to take responsibility for my own life and admit that things might have turned out differently if I had been a better person."

"I want to argue with you about that. Because I think you're an awesome person, but I like that determination to take responsibility for your actions. It's the right way to be."

He opened the church door and held it while the three ladies walked in. Mallie waited for him, and they followed the girls into the sanctuary.

The pastor was waiting, sitting in the front pew, his head bent down like he was either praying or reading something on his lap.

He looked up as he heard their footsteps.

"Ah! The wedding party is here." He looked back down, gathered some papers, and then stood.

Walking down the aisle felt final to Mallie. She wasn't wearing a wedding dress, and her father wasn't giving her away, the pews weren't filled with happy well-wishers, and she didn't have attendants waiting on her near the altar, but it still felt solemn and sober.

Her stomach cramped, and her lungs felt bottomless.

She tried to breathe steadily, although the edges of her vision felt black, and when they got to the front, she said, "Do you mind if I sit down?"

"Are you okay?" Jones asked, and he bent over her, putting a hand on her arm and trying to meet her gaze.

"I'm fine. Just a little nervous. And I'm not backing out, but I'd just like to sit down a little."

"Pastor, is it okay if we have the marriage counseling sitting down?"

The girls came behind them and sat in the second pew. The pastor nodded. "Let me get a chair. You two go ahead and sit there, and I'll just sit in front of you. It doesn't have to be formal."

That was a relief to Mallie. She had been a single mom for so long. That was the way she viewed herself. And now, after hardly thinking about it at all, she was going to be joining her life to this man.

She felt it was a good decision. He had been kind to both of their daughters and had asked her opinion on everything that was happening at the ranch.

He was trying to build it for his sister but, knowing that she was not going to be living in it, was not holding to her wishes with an iron-fast will.

"Can we get a cow?" she asked, causing Jones's eyes to pop wide open.

"A cow?"

"I think Ellen in town sells Highland cows. She and her uncle. I was hoping we could get one."

"Sure," he said, still sounding uncertain.

She smiled. "I'm sorry. I'm just trying to take my mind off thinking about how I feel. I think a little bit of nervousness is normal, and that doesn't bother me at all. But the more I think about how nervous I am, the worse I feel. So, I started thinking about cows."

"I see. You're distracting yourself. How do you girls feel about cows?" he asked, turning around and encompassing both Florence and Toni in his gaze.

She loved that. That it wasn't just about Florence, it was about both of them. They hadn't talked about finances or really anything important. They just spent casual time together, getting to know each other while they waited for the pastor to be ready.

Maybe she should have spent her time learning about him, instead of just getting used to him.

Both girls squealed, and they asked how soon.

"Well, we need to move into the house, so somebody's there to feed them every day. But...next weekend?" He lifted his brows at Mallie.

"Next weekend. Yes. Did you say your sister wanted animals?"

"She did, but I don't want you to have to take care of animals if that's not what you're interested in."

"Oh, I am. I think that will be fun. I think the girls will enjoy it."

The pastor slid his chair over, and they stopped talking, facing forward as he settled himself, opened his Bible, and then folded his hands and looked at the two of them.

"I've been thinking about something, since this is not the first marriage I've performed in the last few years where the couple has decided in a relatively short amount of time to get married. I'm pleased to say that every single marriage that I have performed has remained intact. And I was trying to figure out why. After all, it's not uncommon for people to get divorced these days." He raised his brows, and Mallie nodded, seeing Jones nod out of the corner of her eye.

Unfortunately, divorce was all too common.

"I decided there are many different reasons for this, but I wanted to talk about two today."

He paused, and Mallie held her breath. She really did want to have the very best marriage that she could. And she was eager to hear what the pastor had to say.

"I believe honesty is important. One of the most important things." The pastor looked down at his Bible. "In Proverbs, Scripture says that **lying lips are abomination to the Lord. But they that deal truly are his delight.**"

He looked back up.

"I think, sometimes we think that God just has rules, and we have to follow them. Sometimes we don't realize that the rules He gives us are for our benefit. Either personally or relationally. I think this 'rule' about lying is both. It behooves us in a personal way to tell the truth. We become people of character when we do not allow ourselves to take the easy way out and tell a lie to cover something that might be a little bit uncomfortable."

He tilted his head, as though thinking, and then he said, "Let me give you an example."

He smiled a little and looked at Jones. "Let's say that your wife comes into the room and she asks you how she looks in the outfit that she has on."

Jones snorted as though he realized that a question like that was almost always a trap.

The pastor looked at Mallie. "Do you want your husband to tell you the truth?"

"Yes." She did not have to hesitate with her answer.

"No, really? What if he hates the outfit, and he says it's hideous?"

"That would be a little bit hurtful, but... I guess I'd prefer that he say it a little bit more kindly."

"But you'd prefer that he tell you that he doesn't like the outfit?"

"Yes."

The pastor nodded, and then he looked at Jones. "I think she's right. There is a kinder way to say that. But the temptation is to tell your wife what you know she wants to hear. She bought the outfit, she spent the money, she wants to hear that you like it. Obviously, she cares about your opinion, and she cares about whether you think she looks nice or not, right?"

"I hope so," Jones said.

"So the temptation is to say, you look beautiful in anything. When she didn't ask if she looked beautiful, she asked if you liked the outfit. Now, saying that is not a lie, but you're not answering her question. If you say 'I love it,' that's a lie."

Jones nodded.

"If she finds out that you told someone else that you hated the outfit, or she can tell by the look on your face that you're lying or that you really don't like it, or you even admit it years later, she is going to know that there was a time that you didn't tell the truth. You want your significant other to always say, my husband will tell me the truth. You want her to be able to depend on you to not lie. Even in a case like that where it might be easier."

He looked at Mallie. "You need to be able to handle the truth. I think sometimes women scare men into lying because they don't want to deal with the eruption that they know the truth will cause."

Mallie nodded. She could remember times in her previous marriage where she had done that exact thing.

"If your husband tells you he doesn't like the outfit, and you cry, or your feelings are hurt, or you stop talking to him, or if you say fine, I'll never buy any new outfits again. I'll just ask my friend what she thinks, or something like that. Anything. You're training your husband that you can't handle the truth. Now, I'm not saying that it's your fault if he lies to you. But you do want to be careful that you don't encourage him to want to lie, because of the way you react when he tells you the truth."

The pastor raised his brows, and Mallie nodded solemnly, knowing he was right.

He turned back to Jones. "But still, regardless of the way she reacts, regardless of your desire to avoid an argument or fight or to keep yourself from getting the silent treatment for the evening, you have to be honest. You must be honest. You should be honest in the kindest way you can possibly be honest, but according to God's word, there is no such thing as a 'little white lie.'" The pastor raised his fingers and made air quotes around the words "little white lie."

"A lie is a lie, and it is an abomination to the Lord. Something God can't stand. And He doesn't want us to do it either. The reason being, at least one of them, is so we can trust each other. Your wife needs to know, without a shadow of a doubt, that she can depend on you to be honest, and your husband needs to know the same thing. That there is no way that you would tell them anything that was not true."

The pastor paused, thinking, as though he wanted to say more, but then he nodded his head. "We can talk about that all day, because our society would like you to think that truth is relative and that there are times where a lie is necessary to kind of grease the wheels of society. But that is not biblical. You do not find that anywhere in the Bible. You only find a God who holds fast to the truth and commands us to do the same."

He looked back down at the book in his hands, and then he raised his gaze again. "The other thing that I wanted to talk about, that I feel is essential, and possibly obvious, to the success of a marriage, is commitment."

Mallie nodded. Obviously they had to have commitment.

"You have to think to yourself, this is for life. There is no eject button if things don't go your way. That there is no get-out-of-jail card, or that you can just do something else if it doesn't work out. You have to be committed to the person who's beside you through everything, for the rest of your life. And we kind of say those words lightly, for better or for worse. I can tell you, as a pastor and also as a person, that there're going to be difficult times in your lives. They are going to come."

The pastor laughed a little. "I'm sure my wife can tell you that there have been times in our marriage where she hasn't liked me very much. I can admit, and I'm sure she would be fine with me saying, that there are times in our marriage where I haven't liked her very much either. But neither one of us have ever said the D word, because both of us were committed on our wedding day to staying together. And you have to make that commitment on a daily basis. Over and over again. Sometimes, a marriage degenerates to the point where you are picking up your cross every morning and carrying it for Jesus. Committing to what you said you were going to do, even though it's hard. Maybe one of you will get sick." He paused.

Mallie's stomach turned. That was quite possible. Or hurt.

"You might end up taking care of your spouse for decades. Or longer. Definitely there are going to be bumps in the road. You have to be determined to be committed to handle them together.

You can't not care about how she feels, or what she thinks, or what he wants, or what he does. You have to be committed to putting your spouse and their needs and your compassion and concern for them before anyone else."

The pastor gave a deep sigh.

"Sometimes we feel like we need to impress people that we barely know. We go around, caring more about what those people think about us, and thinking about what we can do for them, than we think about or care about our own family. Both men and women are susceptible to this. I think it's more of a personality type. When you care more about how people perceive you. And you know your spouse already knows everything there is to know about you, so you're not concerned with impressing them. And you spend your energy impressing others. That's a terrible trap to fall into, and you need to be careful to be committed to your spouse, above all others."

The pastor looked back down at his notes, and then he fingered them just a little.

"That's probably the one thing that marriages need more than anything else. Two people who are committed. It's not going to work if just one of you is committed. It's not going to work if just one of you decides you want to have a good marriage, or that you're going to be faithful, or that you're going to be kind and commit yourself to your wife or your husband. It has to be both. Otherwise, it just doesn't work."

The pastor looked up, his brows raised.

Mallie supposed that his words should have scared her a little. Made her even more afraid than she had been, but conversely, they actually strengthened her resolve. The pastor hadn't said a word about love, which was odd, considering it was a wedding. But she supposed two people could be committed to each other without loving each other. It wasn't necessary to have love, the world's definition of love anyway, in order to have a biblical marriage.

They just needed to decide to do what was right and then do it. And let their actions speak louder than their feelings.

"I'm going to say something that you don't often hear in churches, or Christian circles, even though it is in the Bible." The pastor paused, and then he looked straight into Mallie's eyes. "We don't like to hear it, but the Bible was pretty clear that in order to win a crown, you have to finish well. In other words, your finish is more important than your start. Somehow marriages tend to start well, and then they putter out. But the finish is what is important. Galatians 6:9 says, **And let us not be weary in well doing: for in due season we shall reap, if we faint not.** We can't faint, we can't quit. There is no reaping if we quit."

The pastor looked up from his Bible. "We get tired. We get weary. We get fed up. But the important thing is to not quit. That's what commitment is. Not quitting."

He closed his Bible. "Do either of you have any questions?"

Mallie looked at Jones, her brows raised. He glanced over at her and shook his head.

She shook her head as well, and they smiled a little at each other, just small smiles, that said that both of them were still determined to do what they had decided to do.

"All right. Let's go over here and stand together, and girls, if you want to stand with us, you can come or you can stay there."

The girls whispered for a minute, and then they came, Toni standing on Jones's side and Florence standing on Mallie's side.

Jones noticed at the same time she did, and they shared a look of happiness. The girls had decided to switch sides, and Mallie wasn't quite sure why, but she liked what that said. That they were going to support both of their parents and not just the parent whose side they came on.

Maybe if it was possible to take four people who were completely unrelated and put them together into a family, they would be able to do it.

That made Mallie feel a lot better too. Toni was the one who would really want a father, and she felt like Jones would be a great dad, which made her feel like she was making a good decision not just for herself but for her daughter.

She determined in her heart to be the very best mother, or whatever it was that Florence wanted, for Florence.

She wasn't being naïve, and she didn't think that things were just going to go super smoothly, but she hoped that she would be able to weather the bumps.

The wedding was over before she knew it, and while she had been listening to the pastor, she also was thinking about the future and how she wanted the rest of her life to play out. How she wanted her marriage to play out in particular. How she wanted her family to be. And she realized that so much of how she wanted her family to be would depend on how she responded to the hardships that came her way. Even when it didn't seem like they were her fault, it was how she reacted to them that mattered. That other people were going to see and hopefully emulate her example. Eventually.

"I now pronounce you man and wife," the pastor said, smiling at them.

Maybe because they had admitted it was a marriage of convenience and not particularly one of love, he didn't tell Jones that he could kiss his bride, and Jones didn't insist on it.

That was probably something they should talk about too. But Mallie felt that maybe they were doing enough changing, since they were planning on moving things out to the ranch when they got home. A new home, a new family, a new life. Lots of changes and things that they were going to have to get used to.

There'd be plenty of time to talk about everything else at some other point.

Jones paid the pastor, and they walked out of the church together. Jones took Mallie's hand, and Mallie liked the way that linked them together. Making her feel like it wasn't the two of them separately anymore, but it was the two of them becoming one. Creating a family.

Hopefully, they'd made a good decision.

# Chapter 19

"That was a longer day than I was expecting," Jones said, sitting on the front porch swing, listening to the sounds of the night stir around them.

The girls had gone to bed, exhausted, more than thirty minutes before, but he had told Mallie that he was going to sit on the porch for a bit. She asked to join him, which pleased him.

He knew she was tired. They worked all day moving their things, and she had to be exhausted. She worked just as hard as he had, and that was after the stress of the wedding in the morning.

"I'm sorry it wasn't a very romantic day for you," he said as the swing springs creaked lightly under his weight as he shifted it gently with his foot.

Mallie tucked her legs up under her so she was sitting cross-legged on the swing. Her knee just brushed his leg occasionally. "I wouldn't have chosen any other way to spend the day. I'm excited to move out here, and... It's hard to believe that it's ours. I feel like it's yours, if that makes sense."

"I think it probably takes a little bit more time to get used to the idea that what's mine is yours and I assume what's yours is mine." It felt a little bit weird to just assume that.

"Yeah. You hesitated there, and it's weird, isn't it? To just start thinking that somebody else's stuff is yours too."

"But that's what marriage is."

"I agree. Still, there's just a part of me that feels like maybe I don't deserve it."

"Keep working on that, because you definitely do."

She leaned her head back on the swing, and he could almost feel the exhaustion radiating from her.

"You don't have to stay out here. I just... My body is tired, but my brain is still going, you know?"

"I feel the exact same way. I feel nice and tired, almost deliciously tired, but a little bit sore too. But my brain...I want to overthink everything. Did I make the right decision? Was this a mistake? How can I stay committed? How can I keep my determination to stay married through the rest of my life? What are the best things for our girls?"

"Exactly. I had those questions and a hundred more. Because I know my work takes me away from home a lot. And it's going to continue to take me away from home. I wonder if maybe I made the right decision in bringing someone into this. Should I have gotten married when I know I'm not going to be home much? Should we take our girls on tour with us and not worry about whether or not they have a regular school? And a million other questions."

"Maybe rather than thinking about it, we just need to do it," Mallie said softly.

He nodded, thinking that was probably about the best thing they could do. Sometimes the thinking about things made them bigger and harder than they actually were.

"Just a day-by-day thing. Every day, just do the right thing. And pretty soon, it becomes weeks and months and years and decades of doing the right thing."

"That's right. And if you mess up, just start again tomorrow, doing the right thing."

"Yeah." He didn't say anything more, but sometimes he wondered what the right thing was. Should he really go back to touring? Should he try to make it as a solo act? What if he failed? What would Mallie think of him then? And did he really want to leave his family like that?

"So, you know what my sister wanted for the farm, but now that it's yours, what are you thinking?"

"It's ours. And I guess I'd like to talk to the girls about it. But I've always wanted a garden. I think it would be a lot of fun to put one in."

"Then let's do that. I know Flo said she wanted a swimming pool, and I honestly feel like I'd like to rent a backhoe and dig the hole myself."

She shifted on the swing, turning her head to look at him. "Really? You want to run a backhoe?"

"Yeah. Is that so unbelievable?"

"No. I guess I just see you with a guitar in your hands and don't really think you're the backhoe running kind of person. But if it's something you want to do, I think you ought to do it. We could make the swimming pool a family project."

"Do regular people put swimming pools in themselves?"

"Surely there are videos online that would show us how."

They laughed together. There was an online video to show them how to do anything. Probably there was an online video for brain surgery.

"All right. It might not be perfect."

"And that would be part of the fun. The swimming pool wouldn't be perfect, and we'd laugh over it every time we saw the imperfections. We'd know that it was because it was a family project, and even though the swimming pool wasn't perfect, maybe it's just a little bit like our family. You know? We love it despite the imperfections."

"It might not hold water."

"We'll patch it until it does."

"You have a solution for every problem?"

"I think there is. Right? We're not going to let a little thing like a leak stop us from putting in our own swimming pool."

"All right. You could be right. Whatever it turns out to be, we're going to swim in it anyway."

"Unless there's an alligator. I don't swim with alligators."

"Considering that it's North Dakota, I don't think I have to worry about you not swimming in the pool."

They laughed together, and then after they sat for a little while, he started singing a song that had been rolling around in his head.

After a little while, Mallie joined him, and the harmony drifted over the empty fields.

Sweet and soft. He could end every day of his life just like this.

Maybe they needed to talk about where their relationship was going, and maybe they needed to talk about what they should do, what he should do. Mallie should have a say in it, but they were tired, and he didn't want to spend any more time talking about things they couldn't do anything about. Plus, probably the girls should have a say in it as well.

Maybe he should call a family meeting. They'd work on that tomorrow.

# Chapter 20

Jones pulled into the auction barn parking lot.

At breakfast that morning, the family meeting hadn't quite gone as planned, because once someone, he thought it was Florence, recommended they go to the auction as a family that evening, they hadn't really talked about anything else other than what kind of animals they wanted to get for the farm.

Mallie had seemed fine adding a few animals, and while they already planned to get Highland cows from Ellen, they thought they might go to the auction, even if just for the entertainment.

"Sounds like it's started," he said as he took Mallie's hand and they started walking toward the building where people milled around everywhere.

"I think seven o'clock is just the suggested time," Mallie said, looking around and seeming happy. She hadn't said anything about him holding her hand but seemed to like it. He definitely did. It gave him a connection that he didn't feel when he walked beside her without it.

"Uncle Jones?" Flo said from behind him.

"Yeah?" he said easily, not slowing down.

"Toni and I were wondering if we would be able to talk to some people about possibly babysitting their kids for the summer to earn money. I mean, if we could do it at our house?"

He looked over at Mallie. She was the one who was going to have to answer that question. His recording studio was in the basement, and any noise the kids made shouldn't bother it too much. But that was the only issue he could think of.

"I suppose we could try it and see how it works out," Mallie said, shrugging her shoulders. "I like that you're trying to think of ways to earn money and that you're willing to do some work in order to do it. Plus, we have that really cute playset outside and a room that seems perfectly set up for a playroom just off the kitchen."

"That's exactly what we were saying. That if we were little kids, we'd just love to be out on the farm, and if a little kid has their mom working all the time, it would be a lot of fun for them to be able to spend some time out with us," Toni explained.

"That sounds good to me, as long as you two think you can get along. I don't want there to be any arguing," Mallie said.

It made Jones smile. So far, Florence and Toni had gotten along perfectly. But he supposed that it was a pipe dream to think that they would never argue or fight.

"We can make some rules, and then both of us can follow them. Rules like we each have to do the same amount of work, and if we have kids, if one of us gets an hour off, the other gets an hour off and stuff like that."

"Yeah. Stuff to make it fair. But I don't really want any time off. I like to play, and it'll just be an excuse to play and have fun if there are kids there."

"Well, they might make a mess, and then both of you will be responsible for cleaning up," Mallie said in a very serious, motherly tone. Jones didn't smile, but it made him want to. It seemed when a woman had children, she developed a tone that sounded just like a mother.

"Okay. We'll think about it, but if we see someone who we know has a kid and is looking for someone, we can say something to them tonight?"

"It's fine with me if it's okay with you?" Mallie looked at him with her brows raised.

They hadn't explicitly agreed that they wouldn't make any decisions without the other, but he appreciated that that seemed to be the default that they had both fallen into. To him, it was just consideration. If a person was married, your life wasn't really yours anymore, it was a life that was connected to your spouse, and you couldn't just go off and do whatever you wanted to do.

After all, whatever he decided for his life would affect Mallie and the girls, and the same thing went for her. Anything that she decided to do would affect him. It just made sense that they would talk to each other before they made decisions.

He supposed it was just basic consideration.

Regardless, they didn't talk too much as they walked into the sale barn and found seats. He had been afraid that they might have missed most of the sale, not that he was looking to buy much of anything, but he didn't want to bring his family too late. But it looked like they were just getting started, with a bunch of small newborn calves going through the ring.

He wasn't really interested in buying a calf. There would be bottles and milk replacer and stuff like that, and he didn't really know much about it. He wanted one that was already eating grass and he could just put it in the pasture and make sure it had water. But he'd talk to Ellen about that, and he and Mallie and the girls would make a decision together.

They watched as the calves went through the ring, the girls trying to guess the weight before it popped up on the screen.

Most of the time, they were way off, although the more calves that went through, the better they got at it. Which made sense.

They seemed like they were having fun, and he was glad that there was something so close that he could take his family for an evening out.

Even if they didn't decide to buy anything, it was still a fun night.

After the calves were done, there was a break and the girls went and got some cheese fries and a drink.

He and Mallie shared a container of fries between the two of them. She liked hers slathered in cheese, and he ate the ones around the edges.

"At least we're compatible in our cheese fries habits," he commented.

"You noticed that too?" she asked with a laugh.

"I noticed you're leaving the crispy ones for me, and I appreciate the fact that you're being a good little wife tonight."

"A good little wife?" she asked with a raised brow, and then she laughed.

As he turned back toward the ring, he almost gasped.

The ugliest goat he'd ever seen was standing in the middle of it. It had long hair and looked like God had been unable to decide exactly what color He wanted it to be, so He didn't make it all the colors of the rainbow, but black, brown, white, and some form of rusty gray red all splattered through its long- and short-haired coat.

"Wow. I've never seen an animal quite that ugly," Jones commented, feeling bad because it was still an animal who deserved to be loved. But this. It was the kind of goat only a mother could love.

Mallie gave him a look, her brows creased, and he thought it was a look of censure, but then she laughed. "There's something wrong with that comment, but it's so true. I just don't know what to say. Wow." She shook her head, looking back at the goat in the pen.

As he looked, he realized it had a huge potbelly too, which made its legs look like they were about two inches long and its body look way out of proportion compared to everything else. On top of that, despite the longish hair over most of its body, its ribs stuck out, and its head seemed to be about twice the size of a normal goat's head.

Or maybe it was just because it was so skinny.

"But it kind of tugs at your heartstrings in a way, doesn't it?"

"It's so ugly it's...cute."

The auctioneer opened the bidding at hundred dollars, but no one bid.

He went down to eighty, then seventy, and finally, when he was at thirty, Mallie touched Jones's arm. "Jones. I know we hadn't talked about goats at all. We discussed a dog, some cats possibly, and cows. Definitely some horses. But..."

"You feel bad for it too?"

"I do."

"Can we get it, please?" Toni turned around, her eyes pleading. Florence had the same look when she turned around.

He might have been able to resist his wife, although he wouldn't have wanted to, but he couldn't resist the pleading in his girls' eyes.

"Looks like I'm gonna have to pay someone to take it off my hands," the auctioneer said before he said, "Twenty? Who will give me twenty? How about a nice twenty?" he said before he went off on his auctioneer chant.

Jones raised his hand.

The auctioneer didn't even try to get a second bid. He slapped the gavel down on the counter in front of him. "Sold! To the gentleman with the softhearted ladies."

Jones laughed, because that was the truth. He hadn't really given too much of a thought that he was the only man in the house, but...it was true. He had all these ladies looking at him, and he had a feeling that he wasn't going to ever be able to say no to any of them.

"Oh my goodness. I can't believe we have a goat!" Florence said, her hands squeezed together, her face pink with excitement.

Toni's hands clasped Florence's as she said, "I can't believe it either!" They giggled, and then Toni said, "the kids that we babysit are going to love this!"

Jones shook his head.

What in the world had he just done? This was his second rash decision in less than a week. Although, this was far less of a commitment than marriage. Surely the goat wasn't going to live 50 years.

Plus, his wife was a lot nicer to look at. He glanced over at her. Her eyes were shining, her lips turned up. But more than that, she always radiated a peace and happiness that he found to be extremely attractive. He definitely did not mind looking at her, but more than looking at her, there was just a joy in being in her presence.

"What did we just do?" he said low, with laughter in his voice, but also his tone said he couldn't believe it.

"I thought getting married on the spur of the moment was a crazy decision. I'm not sure about our capability of making rational, adultlike decisions together."

"I was having the same kind of concern. Maybe we shouldn't be allowed to go out unsupervised."

"Definitely the girls do not count as supervision," Mallie said in a slightly louder tone.

"Mom! Having a goat is going to be a lot of fun. You just wait."

"Have you ever owned a goat before?" Jones asked as Toni turned back around, waving at her friends who had just come in on the other side of the arena.

"Can we go over and see Sorrell and Merritt?" Toni turned around and asked.

Mallie looked at him, and he nodded.

"Sure. Just don't leave the building without letting us know, okay?" he said.

It made him nervous that he was now responsible for two children. What if he made a mistake? He didn't want to make a bad decision that was going to hurt his kids.

He stuck that in the back of his head, knowing the best thing he could possibly do would be to read his Bible more and try to gain the Lord's wisdom. That would be the one thing that would make him a better husband and father. He never felt such a longing for God, and he supposed that in a way marriage had been good for him already. Since it made him realize that he wasn't as self-sufficient as what he thought he was.

Of course Annika's death had done that as well, but this was a completely different perspective. With two lives depending on him to raise them to be responsible adults.

There he was, having just bought the ugliest animal he'd ever seen in his entire life and thinking about how he was going to try to raise his girls to be responsible adults.

How could he do that when he wasn't one himself?

"Did we just make a big mistake?" he asked again.

"It's going to be just fine," Mallie said with confidence, and he felt like he needed to believe her.

They stayed for more of the auction, but he wasn't tempted to bid on anything else, although it probably helped that his girls weren't there to turn around and ask him to, either. Because there were some cute piglets that came through, and Mallie seemed to look a little bit longingly at them.

But one crazy animal per visit to the auction barn would be more than enough.

Maybe this wasn't such a family-friendly outing after all.

The auction wasn't quite over when he leaned over to Mallie and said, "Should we go down and see what we need to do to get our goat home?"

"Sure." She seemed tired; it had been a big day of arranging their furniture and deciding what else they needed to add. Also they'd unpacked the kitchen, and the workers had realized they'd forgotten to put silicone around the window, so there had been some people coming in and out of their home.

They stood together, greeting their neighbors as they walked to the window to pay, and were directed to go to the loading dock to pick up the goat.

They found their girls still hanging out with Sorrell and Merritt along with their parents. They stopped to chat for a few minutes before they all left together.

"I'm not sure how I feel about taking that thing home in my pickup," he said, looking dubiously behind him as he pulled out of his parking place.

There was plenty of room in the back seat between Toni and Florence, so it wasn't a matter whether or not it would fit. It was a matter of whether or not he wanted his pickup to stink.

"We'll clean it out tomorrow. We promise."

"We can hire someone to bring it out," Mallie suggested.

"We could."

The girls were silent as he thought about it. He appreciated that and decided that he would take them up on their offer.

"All right. I know you guys would like to have it out tonight. And I trust that you'll do your very best to clean the pickup out when we get up tomorrow morning. So, we'll do that."

The girls squealed in the back seat, and Mallie gave him a smile. He felt like he made the decision that she wanted, but he still wasn't super happy about it.

He supposed if he was going to be a farmer, and if he was going to have children, he would have to understand that his pickup wasn't going to stay pristine.

Still, goat poop? He wasn't sure he was ready for that.

But it had made his girls happy, and he would trade goat poop for a smile.

He backed into the dock and handed his ticket to Coleman, who said, "Ah. You're the one who bought that ugly goat." Then he laughed. Jones wasn't sure what to say. It didn't sound like a good laugh.

"Yeah. My girls fell in love with it."

"Or they just felt pity for her. I almost bought her out of pity," Coleman said, shaking his head and laughing again. He sobered. After giving a man standing nearby directions to go get the goat, he said, "She's probably going to have those kids pretty soon. Possibly tonight. That wouldn't shock me, especially with all the excitement that she had."

"Kids?"

"You know. Baby goats are called kids."

"It's pregnant?" Jones felt like he was being a little bit dense, but it hadn't occurred to him, not even a little bit, that the potbelly that he'd been thinking made it look completely out of proportion was a pregnant belly. He felt stupid now.

"You didn't realize she was pregnant?" Coleman asked with a grin. He looked at Mallie. "I'm sorry, but I feel like you might have your work cut out for you. If you need me to talk to him about something, just let me know."

"I would take you up on that, except you probably have to talk to both of us. Because it didn't occur to me that the goat might be pregnant either."

Coleman huffed at that, and Jones put his arm around his wife and hugged her to his side.

She could have made fun of him with Coleman, instead of admitting that she was exactly like he was.

He appreciated that.

"Seriously," Coleman said as they watched the man bring the goat down the aisle. "I wouldn't be surprised if none of the babies make it. She obviously hasn't been getting a whole lot to eat, and I'm not sure if she does have them, whether she'll be able to feed them or not. If you need some help with them, give me a call. If I can't help you, I can hook you up with someone who can."

"All right. I'll keep that in mind."

If there were any problems, he was going to have to get hooked up with someone, since he had no idea of how to handle anything.

"Let me give you Dr. Lark's number too. She or Dr. Mabel can come out if you need them."

"All right. I'll take them."

If the goat was going to have babies, someone who knew something about delivering babies should probably be there.

Owning goats was becoming a little bit more complicated than what he thought.

"Do you have any hay or feed?" Coleman asked as the man stopped in front of them, and the goat looked up at them with liquid brown eyes.

It was ugly but so sweet. Both of his girls stood beside it, petting it, while it stood docile, enjoying their ministrations.

"No. No hay. No feed."

"All right. If you want me to, I can give the feed store a call in the morning and get you an order set up, and you can either pick it up or they'll bring it out."

Coleman looked like he'd helped people with this more than once. And Jones figured he wasn't the first person in the world to buy something at the sale barn and realize that he'd gotten into something a little bit more than what he was expecting.

"If you do, I'd appreciate it. I think once I see what it needs, I'll be able to do it myself."

"Of course. We all have to start somewhere. So don't hesitate to give a shout to anyone if you need help. We've all been there."

"Unless you grew up on a farm."

"That's true. But those people have advantages the rest of us don't."

He hadn't realized that Coleman didn't grow up on a farm, but he didn't stand around and talk about it.

The girls had been moving the goat around the side of the pickup, and now they needed his help to lift her up.

"I'd thank you, but I'm not sure whether you actually did me a favor tonight or not. I'm not sure I'll be back. I thought this would be a nice family evening, but—"

Coleman huffed out a laugh again. "The girls will have you back. Count on it."

"All right. If you say so. I think I'm gonna have three crying females if the babies don't make it."

"Well, that's completely possible, but that's also a fact of life. Sometimes part of life is death. And once she gets her strength back, she might be able to have babies next year."

Jones wasn't sure whether that was a good thing or a bad thing, but he refrained from saying so.

Mallie squeezed his hand, and they bid Coleman good night.

He pulled out of the auction barn, and he couldn't help it—he started to sing. The girls joined in, and Mallie knew the song too, and before they'd turned off the main highway, they were all singing it at the top of their lungs.

*There was a goat*
*Now please take note*
*There was a goat*
*There was a man*
*Who had a goat*
*He loved that goat*
*Indeed he did*
*He loved that goat*
*Just like a kid.*

*One day that goat*
*Felt frisk and fine*
*Ate three red shirts*
*Right off the line*
*The man, he grabbed*

*Him by the back*
*And tied him to*
*A railroad track.*

*Now, when that train*
*Drove into sight*
*That goat grew pale*
*And green with fright*
*He heaved a sigh*
*As if in pain*
*Coughed up those shirts*
*And flagged the train!*

Maybe the singing was worse than he thought, or maybe it was just time. But no sooner had he pulled onto the side road, when one of the girls said, "I think our goat is having babies."

# Chapter 21

**"I** 'm sorry I couldn't save them," Lark said as she wiped her hands on a rag she pulled from the back pocket of her coveralls.

"No, it's okay. Coleman told me that there was a good chance they wouldn't make it."

Jones's voice held deep sorrow and deep exhaustion.

Mallie went over and put her arm around him, leaning into his side and allowing him to lean into her.

Immediately his arm came around her, and it was like the burden was instantly halved when they were facing it together.

The girls had gone to bed a while previously, when the first goat had been born dead.

Lark had suggested that the other ones wouldn't have any better fate, and the girls didn't want to see that.

He and Mallie had stayed until the end.

"Are you going to milk her?" Lark asked as she rinsed the bucket out with the hose at the opening of the barn.

"Milk her?" Mallie said, surprised. She hadn't even considered that. But she supposed that was just one of the many things they hadn't considered.

"She's really thin and very malnourished, but if you feed her a good diet, she'll come back. Her milk will be good either way, after a couple of days, once you get the colostrum out."

Mallie looked up at Jones, who seemed just as surprised as she was that the goat might need to be milked.

"It's not a necessity?" Jones asked.

"It's not. It would be good for her in some ways to have an entire year of rest, but at the same time, it's an entire year. She could be supplying you with milk to drink, or to make soap with, or there are other products people use it for."

"So you don't give a recommendation either way?"

"I think it will probably be best for her, if you're going to keep her and breed her again, for you to milk her. That's the natural thing that happens. And you don't know that you might not end up with kids somewhere that you could feed. But it's totally up to you. That's quite a commitment."

Mallie nodded. "It has to be done every day?" she asked, knowing that probably wasn't a smart question, but she truly didn't know the answer.

"You can do it every day, or most people do it twice a day. But once a day might be good for her."

"I see." She sighed.

As though Jones could feel her exhaustion, he said, "Maybe we'll sleep on that and make a decision tomorrow."

"That'll be fine. There's no need to do it now." Lark gave them a few more instructions on what they needed to do with her, gave him some instructions on what she would like to see her eat, which Jones said he would consult with Coleman and make an order at the feed store, and then Lark climbed wearily into her truck and drove off into the night.

Jones closed the barn door behind her, and then he stood beside Mallie and watched her taillights disappear down the driveway.

"That wasn't exactly how I was expecting to spend most of the evening," Jones said.

"Me either. But I don't really regret it."

"Really?"

"I mean, seeing those little babies not breathing..." She shuddered and didn't say anything more. "That was hard. It was hard to see the girls' disappointment. But I guess it was a baptism by fire, you know? If we're going to have animals, if we're going to do this ranch thing, they're not going to be the last animals we lose. We survived, and we'll be stronger because of it."

Jones nodded, thinking about what she said. And then he put his arm around her, tugging gently, and she came in toward him.

"I guess I kind of see what you're saying. I didn't like what we're doing, but I liked that I was doing it with you. It's...a bonding experience maybe?"

She nodded. That's kind of what she was saying too. It made them see that together they could handle it. "Yeah. I mean, I suppose you can always handle more than what you think you can, but the idea that we did together. Yeah."

He felt solid and strong beside her, and she had admired his steadiness all evening. Both of them were doing something they had never done before, and there hadn't been any hysterics, any arguments or harsh words. And Jones had felt like someone who could handle all the bad news and keep working until the situation was resolved. Even if it took until two o'clock in the morning.

They'd laughed together, they'd sung together, and they'd had a good evening overall, besides the loss of the three small kids. At least the mom was doing well.

"We'll have to think of a name for her tomorrow."

"I'm sure the girls will have ideas."

"I'm sure they will too. We never heard whether they got any babysitting clients or not."

"Yeah, the goat kind of took over everything."

"That might be the way animals are. At least emergencies."

"Yeah. I'm glad that Lark was able to come out. And I'm glad you were there. I thought to myself that I wouldn't want to have anyone else beside me. You made it...maybe not fun, but good." He walked up the porch steps beside her and opened the door so she could walk in first.

They'd already washed their hands up at the barn, and as they climbed the stairs together, she had to admit that she was looking forward to a shower and going to bed.

"You know I keep thinking that I want to talk to you about our relationship, and the way things are going, but then something comes up, and I never get a chance to."

"Yeah. We probably should talk. I have some things I need to do with my business, and I want you and the girls to help me make the decision. But again, it seems like I keep thinking I want to do it, but no good time ever comes up."

She stopped at the top of the stairs; her room was to the left, and his to the right.

They hadn't really talked about it, other than when the girls picked their rooms, she had said "and I'll take this one," and he had walked into a different room.

That had hurt her heart just a little, that they hadn't even said anything about it. It made her feel like maybe he wasn't expecting their marriage to include sharing a room. But he held her hand and put his arm around her, and that made her think that maybe he was hoping for more.

She didn't know, and she hated guessing. She wasn't a great guesser and figured she would assume the wrong thing anyway.

"Tomorrow. Let's decide that we're going to sit down and talk about everything tomorrow." Jones raised his brows, as though asking if that was okay with her.

"That sounds good. We'll put it all out in the open. Some of the things, the girls need to give their input on, and maybe you and I need to have a little bit of time where we talk about things privately."

He had to understand that she meant their relationship, and he nodded.

"Tomorrow's another day." He paused, and then he said, "Thanks for spending today with me."

"And thank you. I had a good time." And she found, despite the sadness and loss, that the good far outweighed the bad, and every word was true. She had enjoyed her day with him, and she would do it all over again in a heartbeat.

# Chapter 22

Jones had every intention of talking with his family the next day, but because they had all been up late, they all slept in, and they hadn't even had breakfast when there was a knock on the door around ten AM.

"Are you expecting anyone?" he asked Mallie who had been standing at the counter cracking eggs into a bowl when he walked in the kitchen.

Lines creased her brow. "I can't think of anyone. The workmen knock sometimes, but I wasn't expecting anyone today."

"Me, either. They were waiting on a couple of parts to get here before they could finish plumbing the basement."

He had talked to the foreman the previous day, and he'd expected them to be completely finished and out of the house by the end of the week.

As he walked to the front door, he could see through the window that it was a car he didn't recognize sitting in the drive. A convertible.

Actually, it looked a little familiar, since it was lime green. He'd seen it before...

When he opened the door, immediately he recognized his good friend and fellow recording artist Bobby, along with his lovely wife Jonna.

"Bobby!" He held out his hand before it dawned on him that Bobby was holding a crockpot.

Jonna had both hands full holding a box that looked to be filled with smaller containers.

"We heard you got married, and we wanted to bring you a wedding gift," Jonna said as Jones stepped back from the door and they walked inside.

"How did you hear that?"

"Sebastian told us," Bobby said, naming the agent they shared.

Bobby was a professional recording artist and music superstar in his own right. He stepped back away from the limelight when he married Jonna over twenty years ago. Carving out time for family had been important to him, and he had given up the huge success he might have been able to be because spending time with his wife and new family had been important.

"So we brought you a housewarming gift, which is the crockpot. But we didn't want to bring it empty, so I filled it with my Pork Colorado and I'm holding the toppings. Supper is on us tonight."

"And you're staying for it, right?" Jones said as he led them to the kitchen.

"We can't. We're just passing through. We're heading toward Florida, where we're going to meet our cruise ship. We're taking a cruise to Panama for two weeks later this month."

"Wow. That sounds like fun."

"It's something I've always wanted to do, and Bobby surprised me with it for our twenty-first wedding anniversary."

"What she's not telling you is that I forgot our twentieth wedding anniversary."

"He didn't forget, he was just sidetracked because one of our grandchildren was born two days before, and neither one of us remembered it. So, we're going big for the twenty-first. No one says you have to celebrate the way everyone else in the world celebrates, right?" Jonna said with a smile that showed that she enjoyed rolling through life as it came.

Jones wondered if that's the way his relationship with Mallie would be in twenty years. More smiles than tears and an easy camaraderie between them.

Taking time out of a cross-country trip to take a meal to a friend.

He stepped into the kitchen. "This is my wife, Mallie. Mallie, this is a good friend of mine and fellow singer, Bobby and his wife Jonna."

"Oh! It's so nice to meet you."

Mallie hurried over to take the box from Jonna's hands and give her a hug.

Meanwhile, Jones continued to explain, because even though Mallie had immediately embraced his friends, she was probably confused.

"They're on their way to meet a cruise ship. Bobby and I have the same agent, so they heard about our marriage and wanted to bring us supper."

"Okay. Well. So you—"

"Bought a crockpot and the ingredients for Pork Colorado, and I put it together before we came. It's not hard, and now all you have to do is plug it in, turn it on low, and supper will be ready this evening." Jonna smiled. "My family loves it, and it was the best thing I could think of to make for you."

"Wow. So nice of you to take the time to stop and to give us a gift and a meal."

"Well, Jones has been a good friend. I know he's gone through some hard times. But he is a solid friend and a solid example for anyone looking after him. I also wanted to meet his wife and family, so there was that."

"And we're in no hurry. We're just casually driving across the country from our home in Oregon."

"Your dad's not with you guys?" Jones asked, knowing that a lot of times Jonna's dad had toured with Bobby, back in the day. Before he quit touring for good.

"Not this time. It's a couple's time. But he's taking care of our dog."

"And he taste-tested the Pork Colorado. It has his stamp of approval as well."

They laughed together, and Jones asked Bobby if they had some time to go out and check out the barn.

"If you don't mind, I'm gonna stay in the kitchen with Mallie," Jonna said.

"Actually, if you know anything at all about gardening, I'd really love some advice. I've been trying to figure out where to put mine, and I'm just not sure."

Jones laughed as the ladies started talking about their gardens, and he figured it was fine for him and Bobby to pop over to the barn. He had a few things he wanted to ask Bobby.

Bobby had successfully navigated the music world as well as having a solid relationship with his wife, and Jones was hoping he would have some advice for him.

They walked out the side door and started toward the barn.

"Where is Florence?"

"Well, I can show you what we were doing last night in the barn, but the short story is, we bought a goat at the auction, and she started having her babies on the way home. So we were all up pretty late last night."

"Baby goats? They're cute."

"Unfortunately, none of them made it," Jones said, not really wanting to get into it but knowing that at least that much had to be said.

"That's sad."

"Yeah. But the mom is still alive. Anyway, the girls were up pretty late, and everybody slept in this morning."

"It's nice when you have a job where you can start whenever you want to."

"Exactly. That's kind of what I wanted to talk to you about. You know how Sebastian is. He's been on me to get started recording and touring and... I'm just not sure. I know you walked that line, where you had people on you who wanted you to keep recording and keep touring, and you had to balance that with having a family and spending time with your wife."

"Well, it's important that you're thinking about this. I'm impressed. Some people don't realize how hard the life of being a star in the spotlight can be on a family. A lot of times, we are too busy reaching for our goals and trying to be bigger and better, and we don't stop to think about how our actions are affecting our relationships."

"That's what I want to try to avoid," Jones said as he opened the door and showed Bobby the goat.

"That thing is ugly," Bobby said.

"That was my thought exactly when I first saw her. Only she had a potbelly, too. Actually, she still has a belly, it just isn't quite as big as it used to be last night."

"Yeah, I'm sorry about the kids. That's hard."

"Yeah. But if you're going to do this ranch thing, you know you gotta take the good with the bad."

"Those are good life lessons. Even though you see success as a singer, there are a lot of disappointments and hardships along the way. The girls might as well learn about them now."

"That's what I was thinking. I was bummed at first, that I had gotten something that caused them pain. But... It's good for them to go through those hard things. Even though it's hard to watch and hard to go through with them."

"Exactly."

They stood by the goat stall, Jones putting a foot on the bottom rail and leaning his forearms on the top as she came over and Bobby scratched her ears.

"Probably the fact that you are concerned about it is the very best thing. Some people don't realize and never do. But beyond that, you know that things are a lot different now than they were even twenty years ago."

"I know. But touring is still touring."

"I know. And you're right about that. And there will always be a demand for people to tour. But you're at the point where you can set your own schedule. You don't have to tour when they want you to."

"You mean only tour when the girls are in school?"

"Or only tour in the summer and take them with you. Of course, if you're going to have animals on the farm, you're gonna have to figure out who's going to take care of them while you're gone." Bobby looked up, his brows raised, and Jones admitted that he was right. The goat wasn't the only animal they were planning on having.

"Annika always wanted to have a lot of animals on the farm. Mallie and I talked about getting more. But you're right. If we're all going to tour together, somebody's going to have to feed them."

"You can hire someone. Same as you can hire someone to cook or clean or whatever. But it's not really a family thing if you hire a person to do it for you."

"Yeah. I wasn't too interested in that."

"But you don't have to leave at all."

"How?"

"Well, like I said, things are different. Not just the way music is consumed, but the fact that there is social media. People are seeing success having YouTube channels, or other videos, or doing Facebook live. Even creating your own website and streaming from there. The possibilities are endless. You can even have fans play with you. If you do a Zoom call or something. You don't have to do things the traditional way."

Jones figured that somewhere in the back of his head he knew that, but the idea that a star recorded their music and then went on tour was just kind of cemented into his mind. That's the way Annika had done it, and that's the way he had planned to do it as well, but Bobby was right. That wasn't the way he had to do it.

"We have our own recording studio here."

"There you go. You don't have to use it to record. You can use it to perform. Or you can set things up outside. You've got the farm, use it as a backdrop. Sing the kind of music that goes with the life that you're living. You don't have to sing any specific thing. You can create your own sound. Now is the perfect time to deviate a little bit from what you and Annika did, to make the music your own."

He just had to admit that everything Jones was saying made perfect sense to him.

"Why stop there? Make it a family affair. You and Annika were a brother-sister duo, even if people didn't always realize that the fellow singing harmony with her was her brother. Why not get your whole family involved? Everyone. Do they sing?"

"I guess they all sing to a certain extent." He wasn't sure how Mallie would feel about that. She already expressed doubts about being in the spotlight. Plus, he'd been trying to protect Florence from the publicity, not expose her to it. "I don't know if I want my family out there like that. I know for a fact that Mallie was uncomfortable with the spotlight. She expressed as much to me. I haven't decided what to do about it, and we need to talk, but I hardly think she's going to want to be part of the band."

"What if you just sang here? What if you didn't go anywhere? You have enough followers that you might be able to start something, completely online, and make enough money to make it worthwhile. Or at least have enough followers to satisfy your need to perform. It's not like you need money."

"That's true. What I made with Annika is more than enough. And I wondered about that too. I… I can't imagine myself not doing anything. I want to do something. I'm too young to retire." He laughed.

"Well, I can totally understand that. But you might need to talk to some people, find some folks who can help you with sound and lighting...and other things, but there may be various places around the farm where you guys can record and just make music. A family thing. No need for publicity of crowds and no need to ever leave the farm. Record it just like that. In fact, if you say that your farm is in North Dakota, it's big enough that people won't find you. You have your privacy, but you also have something that your family did together."

"The girls would probably never forget growing up and singing with their parents."

"And it would bind you together... Sometimes trying to put a second family together is hard."

Jones knew that Bobby spoke from experience, and he nodded, admitting that Bobby was most likely right, bowing to his wisdom and experience.

"Probably the most important thing is to find something that satisfies you but also keeps your wife happy. The two of you need to do it together. And both of you need to be satisfied with the way things are going. And it might be a good idea to check in occasionally with each other as well, making sure that your goals and aspirations haven't changed. Sometimes you drift apart and you don't even know it."

"I can see the danger there." And there would be an especially big danger if he had fans and music execs pulling him in one direction and ended up going with them, thinking that Mallie was behind him but never checking.

"I know you know this, man, but fame, fortune, all of that. It comes and goes. But family, they're the ones that will be here for the long haul, as long as you take care of them. But you can't expect them to be around if you constantly neglect them."

Jones nodded, and then their conversation turned to news of the music business before they took a last look at the goat, who still didn't have a name, and walked out the door toward the house.

# Chapter 23

"If I put it here, it will be closer to the house, and I can just picture me coming out in the morning and picking some spinach for our omelets, you know?" Mallie said, showing Jonna the plot of ground where she had been hoping to put her garden.

"Anything that makes it easier will probably make it more likely that you continue to do it. So as long as there is sufficient sunlight," Jonna said, looking up at the sky and squinting to figure out which direction would give them the best angle. "I think it's a good idea."

"I agree," Mallie said, and then she paused and glanced around before she said, "Has it been hard being married to someone who is gone a lot? I mean, I'm asking because Jones is taking a trip to Tennessee, and he's going to be gone for almost a week. I've been dreading it, to be honest."

Jonna gave her a knowing look. "When Bobby and I got married, Bobby had to make a decision. He was probably not at the height of his career, but he was on a fast upward trajectory, and he had people clamoring from every side for him to do more, be more, give more, expose himself more. More tour dates, more recording, just to feed the frenzy and still get as big as he could. You know it's all about money." Jonna shrugged her shoulder like that was common knowledge.

"So he and I had a long discussion, and he decided that his family was more important. He didn't exactly give up his career, but he basically walked away from what could have been superstar status. We haven't had to live on a shoestring budget, but we've been careful, and we've been very happy. I don't think he regrets that decision, and I know I definitely don't."

"I hate the idea that Jones might have to give that much up for me. I don't want him marrying me to be the hardest and worst decision he's ever made."

"I don't think it will be. Especially if you are a happy, fun person to be around."

Mallie considered that. She didn't think of herself as a bubbly, fun person. In fact, she was more on the quiet, serious side. But there wasn't any rule that said she couldn't change, that she couldn't try to smile more. Who didn't enjoy being around someone who was cheerful? And just because she was cheerful didn't mean she had to suddenly become a great conversationalist, when that wasn't really her thing.

She tucked those thoughts away to think about later. Because the Bible talked about the joy of the Lord making a person strong. Obviously, joy was a biblical concept and not necessarily a personality trait.

Interesting.

"Ultimately, the two of you will have to do what works for your family. But in order for you to stay together, I would highly recommend spending as much time together as you can. I know modern wisdom, using that word loosely," she said with a grin, "says that you need your alone time, but I have a tendency to disagree. God meant for families to work together, play together, eat, sleep, and worship together. Now, we have a tendency to go after our own things, having our own interests, and show up at the supper table, being almost complete strangers."

"I have to agree with that."

They looked around beside the house and saw the men coming from the barn.

"I don't know what Bobby's going to say, but I think we need to head out. We have a lot of driving to do to get to the other side of the country."

They talked for a little bit more, and as Jonna had suspected, they left shortly after.

Mallie felt like she had a lot of things to think about and even more things that she wanted to discuss with her husband. Maybe, they could finally have that talk they'd been trying to have for a while.

# Chapter 24

"Can we go pick out our cow today?" Flo said as they were sitting around the breakfast table eating the omelets he and Mallie had put together after Bobby and Jonna had left.

It surprised him that the death of the goat kids last night hadn't turned her against animals.

"We are afraid Bella will be lonely."

"Bella?" he asked, glancing at Mallie to see if she had any idea what they were talking about.

"The goat," Flo said like it was obvious.

"Bella is Spanish for beautiful." Mallie's lips twitched, but to her credit, she did not smile.

He did not snort out a laugh but caught it before it made its way out of his throat, although it felt like there was a boulder wedged there, in order to keep it down.

Bella was anything but beautiful.

"All right. Bella probably will be lonely. Goats are herd animals, and I do believe I've heard somewhere that you shouldn't keep them by themselves."

"And she would have had three babies, and now she's sad. So, since we were going to get cows anyway, Flo and I decided that today would be a good day. If that's okay with you guys," Toni said, looking cute and sweet as she stared at him across the breakfast table.

This was something he was going to have to talk to Mallie about too. He was pretty much mush every time the girls looked at him.

She was going to have to be the one with the backbone of the family. He was going to have to make sure he told her that.

"Mallie?" he asked, raising his brows and wondering if she would be any voice of reason today, since both of them seemed to fail at that yesterday.

He thought that kind of tongue in cheek, because he didn't really think they were failures. He didn't regret getting the goat, and he didn't regret what happened afterward, other than he would have been much happier to see the babies born alive. But obviously his girls were practicing compassion and consideration, and he couldn't complain about that.

"I'm fine with it. Although, I do believe you have to leave on your trip soon?"

"That's true. I need to leave tomorrow. Maybe we should wait to get cows until I come back." He looked at the girls. "Do you guys think you can keep Bella," he managed to say that with a straight face, "company until I get back next week?"

"Sure. Are we allowed to sleep in the barn?"

"There might be mice, but I don't care," Mallie said with her brows raised.

"I'm fine with it. If you girls want to. Although, I have some tents in the basement, and you might be more comfortable in the yard. I...don't want to scare you out of the barn, but I did see a mouse in there yesterday."

"Yuck!" the girls said. "We'll sleep in the tents. Is it okay if Bella sleeps with us?"

"Sure. There's a big one and a little one, and probably both of you could fit in the big one."

"Us and the goat?" Toni asked, as though making sure.

"Sure. But I don't think goats are potty trainable, so just be aware."

"Oh. That reminds me, we have to clean up the pickup today."

"Before you do that, I had a couple of things I wanted to ask you guys. Maybe you can think about them, because then I want to talk to Mallie."

Both of the girls had started to pick their plates up, but they stopped as he spoke, and their eyes were wide and concerned as they settled back into their chairs.

"It's nothing bad. It's just...a family meeting."

"That sounds serious," Toni said slowly.

"And scary," Florence added.

"I don't think it should be either. I have some decisions I have to make, and I wanted both of you to have some input in them. Unless of course you don't care."

"Maybe. What decisions are you talking about? Do you want us to quit school and live in the jungle?" Toni asked, grinning, like that would be a grand adventure.

"If you didn't like the mice in the barn, you probably won't like the snakes in the jungle," he said.

"Right. Snakes are bad. North Dakota is nice, because there aren't very many snakes."

"I can agree with that," Mallie said with a grin.

"I think everyone agrees with that," Jones said, because he sure did. He wasn't afraid of snakes, but he didn't particularly care for them. And he suspected that if they found one, he would be the one who would have to dispatch it.

Unless he wasn't there.

He didn't like that idea.

"I haven't gotten a chance to talk to Mallie about this, so if she has an aversion to any of it, we're going to defer to her." He raised his brows at the girls, who nodded. He wasn't entirely sure they understood completely what he was saying, but they didn't argue. "I have to travel. I'm leaving tomorrow, and I'll be gone for five days at least. Part of my job is traveling a lot. And I'm not sure how you guys feel about that. I can...choose to do something else that will help me be home more often. I can try to adjust my schedule so that you guys can go with me, or we can figure out something to do with all of us together."

Mallie's eyes got big, and he guessed she was probably trying to keep herself from vehemently disagreeing. She hadn't wanted any part of the fame and fortune, hadn't wanted any part of being in the spotlight, and he could read that easily on her face.

"Bobby said that we could probably do something online. Never having to leave the home, and never having to have people come here. They would just watch us online. It would take some time to build an audience, and it would also not be a guarantee of success."

"You mean we would sing as a family and post it online?" Florence asked, who had more of an idea of what he was talking about than Toni did, since he wasn't even sure Toni knew what he did for a living.

"Sure. That's exactly what I'm saying. I would write some songs, maybe Mallie would help me." He lifted his brows at her, and she didn't shake her head, so he thought maybe she was open to the possibility. "And then we practice them and perform them. Of course, we could always perform hymns or covers, but probably the best thing to do would be to have a mixture of all of those things."

"I like singing hymns together on the porch. That is fun. I don't know if I want people videotaping me while I sing though." Toni bit her lip.

"That's something we'll have to think about. And something I need to talk to your mom about."

"But if we did that, I would be able to stay home all the time. We'd be able to have lots of animals, and we'd be here all the time to take care of them. And Toni and I will be able to go to school and keep seeing Sorrell and Merritt and all of our other friends."

"Exactly. You'd have a normal life, except we'd probably be practicing a lot of music in the evenings and on weekends. But if you enjoy singing together, it shouldn't be too hard or odious."

"Odious?" Florence wrinkled up her nose.

"Something that you don't like. Basically something that smells bad."

No one said anything for a couple minutes, and the girls seemed to think for a bit.

He didn't want to keep them from cleaning out the pickup, so he said, "You girls can get up and go. Your mom and I'll clean off the table while we chat. You're going out to clean the pickup, right?"

They nodded, grinned, and then hopped up and ran out the door.

"Toni is loving her time on the farm. I know we lost the babies last night, but the girls came down this morning, a little bit sad but mostly excited. And I love that they can't wait to go outside. And they have so many plans and things that they want to do," Mallie said as she stood and started to gather the plates from the table.

"I'm sorry we didn't get a chance to talk about things before I popped it on the girls. But I figured it wouldn't hurt to lay out some options for them."

"No, I don't think they'll get their hearts set on any one thing, although they did seem pretty excited to be able to stay here full time. And I have to admit I'm not real excited about you leaving."

"I'm not excited about leaving either. In fact, I've been dreading it. And... I've never dreaded it before."

"I hope I wasn't a bad influence on you, but I'm glad that I'm not the only one who's kind of dreading it."

"I haven't really had to leave too much since Annika's accident. Maybe I have gotten spoiled. Or maybe it was just before, with Annika and Flo, they weren't... They weren't a wife," he ended lamely. He didn't know how to explain it. He did feel protective toward and had loved his sister, but it wasn't the same way he felt for his wife.

He didn't like to examine his feelings too much. Didn't even really want to talk about them, but it was just different. And he didn't know how to put that into words.

"Yeah. It's funny because I've spent over a decade by myself. And yet, the idea of being alone is not exactly scary but definitely not appealing. And yet, I know I can do it. I've done it for years. I have been wondering what's wrong with me."

"Maybe it's just the way it happens when you get married. You have an attachment to the other person. And that maybe is common sense, but it's taken me by surprise."

"Maybe because of the way we got married. It was just supposed to be a marriage of convenience." She took a breath, like the next thing she was going to say was hard. "Which is something I wanted to talk to you about too," she said as she set the dishes down in the sink.

"Our marriage?" he asked, and he couldn't help the shudder of fear that shivered up his backbone. Surely she wasn't changing her mind.

"I... We never really talked about us. What we expected from us."

He wanted to scratch his head. He expected commitment, like the pastor talked about, and faithfulness. He expected her to be a mother to Florence and he would be a father to Toni. He wasn't sure what else she was thinking.

Maybe she read the confusion on his face.

"Our relationship. I wasn't sure what our relationship was, or what it was going to be. You...hold my hand, and...I like that." She turned toward the sink and turned the water on, rinsing off the plates before setting them in the dishwasher.

She liked him holding her hand. And she was a little embarrassed to admit it, or at least that's what it seemed like since she turned her back while she said it.

He had to take a minute to smile. The idea that she enjoyed holding his hand just did that to him. "If it means anything, I enjoy holding your hand too."

"Of course it means something," she said, without turning back around.

He carried the skillet over and set it on the stove before he took a step and put a hand on her shoulder.

"Mallie?"

"Yes," she said without stopping her work.

"Look at me."

She shut the water off and turned. "Are you...asking how I feel about you?"

He didn't know why he was pushing her, he didn't want to push himself, except she had said she liked holding his hand, and he wanted to kind of examine that. It made him feel good, and maybe there was more she liked.

"I guess. Or... I'm not sure."

"What are you expecting from me in terms of a relationship and that type of thing?"

"What do you expect?"

"I guess I kind of felt like I shouldn't expect anything. After all, if you have expectations that aren't realistic, sometimes you feel let down."

"That's right. I don't want to let you down."

"You wouldn't!" she said, her face sincere.

He grinned. "That's the way I feel. About you."

"No expectations? Or like I won't let you down?"

"Both."

"I see." She was quiet, her eyes fixed on a spot on his neck.

"I guess we still haven't figured anything out though."

"No. I guess we haven't."

"All right. I guess I'll go first. I...wasn't sure what I was thinking when I asked you to marry me. Mostly that you would probably say no, and I would have done what I told Florence I was going to do. I didn't really give a thought to romance. But now, I feel like the more I get to know you, the more I like you. I like your character, anyway; you're happy all the time, and how you're willing to roll with things, for the most part. Although, I could see the panic on your face when we talked about performing in public."

"I was trying to hide it."

"I could see that." He grinned, knowing that not everyone had grown up in the spotlight the way he had. Since he and his sister had been seen since they were teenagers. They sang at fairs and in churches and anywhere anyone would give them an opportunity across the country.

"It's not that I'm not willing to learn." She didn't sound real excited about it, but he appreciated that about her. Appreciated that she seemed to have a level head on her shoulders, even if she did allow him to buy the ugliest goat they both ever saw last night.

"But I guess we keep getting off the subject."

"That's partly my fault. I've been dreading talking about it, but I wanted to. We probably should have talked before we got married, although whatever we decide won't affect how I feel about our marriage."

"Me, either. I made a commitment, I plan to stick to it. But I would like to have a...romantic relationship with my wife." He wasn't sure how else to word that, he didn't want to scare her away, but he also didn't want her to doubt what he was saying.

"Yeah. I chose a bedroom, and you chose a separate one, and—"

"I didn't want to push you. I didn't want to scare you either."

"I appreciate it. I really do. I wasn't trying to say that we should change things, not yet anyway, but that just made me wonder what exactly you were expecting."

"I see. I think it's always easier whenever we have a clear idea of what the other person is thinking anyway."

"Yeah. And I guess I was thinking that this would be a marriage where we share a room, but maybe we just need to get to know each other first?"

"I hadn't even put it in those terms, but that sounds good to me. I guess I was just hoping for more but figured that it wouldn't really be up to me."

"And why wouldn't it?" she asked, looking truly confused.

"I don't know. It just seems like the woman always leads in that area."

"Oh. Well, I don't really want to. I mean, I guess this is just something that I'd like for us to do together along with everything else."

"Okay. You mean, you don't want to make all the moves?" he asked with a small grin, like he was teasing her just a bit.

"We might never get anywhere if I'm the one that is supposed to be making all the moves. I am so out of practice it's not even funny. And actually, that's not even really true. I've never been very good at making moves."

"Moves like this?" he asked, stepping closer and sliding an arm around her waist.

She didn't pull back, and he saw that as a good thing. She actually looked up and grinned. "Is that a move?"

"It is. Pretty slick, wasn't it?"

"I don't think I want you to do all the moves you've been practicing on everyone else on me."

He laughed. "I was teasing you. I certainly have not practiced any moves. If anything, the opposite is true. I'm better at getting away from women than I am at getting close to them."

"You run from women?"

"In my line of work, sometimes it's necessary. There are ladies who...follow the band around."

"That's interesting, since your sister was the head of the band. You'd think that there'd be a lot of men hanging around."

"I guess there's ladies who follow her, and someone in the band catches their eye."

"You're quite handsome, so I can see how you would catch someone's eye."

"Quite handsome?" he asked, lifting his brows, wondering if she would give him a better compliment.

"Well, those deep brown eyes are definitely soulful and romantic. And what girl doesn't love a man who sings?"

"Keep going. I'm listening."

"Oh. I wasn't done?"

"Were you?"

"Well, I suppose if they see you with Florence, that will melt their hearts too."

"Like it does yours?"

"So you're making me make all the moves?" she said instead of answering his question.

"I like it when you sing with me. I like harmonizing. I like that you're not always trying to steal the spotlight. Some people do. They can't do anything but sing lead."

"Some people are born to sing lead."

"That's true. Like Annika. She most definitely was, but... She was my sister, and I wasn't trying to have a marriage with her."

"Thankfully." She laughed.

"Aren't you going to ask me for more?" he teased her, since he had pushed her.

"No. I want your compliments to be natural and organic."

He snorted at her gentle teasing. "All right. I like your omelets."

"The way to a man's heart is through his stomach."

"I like to think I'm more than my stomach."

"It might be true, but it could be your ego talking too."

He snorted. "I like that you're not going to allow me to take myself too seriously."

Her face sobered. "I really do like you. And I really do like laughing with you. I like that I can tease you and you tease me back, but not in a mean way."

"I like that you laugh. I've been with some women who don't seem to have that ability, at all."

"I like that you like it. You don't think I'm silly or irresponsible."

"The only time I had doubts about your ability to be responsible was when you allowed me to buy that goat."

"Bella. Beautiful. Our beautiful goat."

"Talk about a name that doesn't fit."

"But she has a beautiful heart," Mallie said, and he snorted at that.

"All right. So, we got that straightened out anyway. The relationship thing?"

"Yes. We're just going to take it slow and see where it goes."

He kind of wanted a bit more of a commitment from her. Maybe a timeframe or the idea that they were developing a romance, but he couldn't argue with that. It was a good start anyway.

He stepped back, and she turned back to the sink.

"What about my job? How do you feel about that?"

"I feel like you need to do what works for you. And we will make it work for us."

"But if you got to choose?"

"I would choose to have you home. Even if that means the family sings with you. Whatever that looks like. Unless you're not going to be happy doing that." She stopped and looked at him. "I'm serious. I can see myself being happy here, raising the girls, possibly working from home again, although... I think I'd like to spend some time gardening and working on the farm, and helping the girls with the animals that they want to get. So, unless you really want me to work, I think that would be my preference for me. And if I get to do what I want to do, I think you should too."

He stood staring at her, appreciating the fact that she wasn't going to dictate to him what she wanted him to do. That she basically told him that she would be happy no matter what.

"What about the girls?"

"Well, we can see what they say, but it sounded to me like they would be happy here, but Florence especially understood that sometimes touring requires you being away, and I think that we would all rather be with you than here alone waiting on you. Maybe the idea that you had of doing your touring while the girls aren't in school was a good one."

"I probably can't arrange it so all the touring happens in the summer, but I might be able to get it so the bulk of it happens. But I guess I'm leaning more and more toward staying home." He grinned. "You think you can handle having me underfoot all the time?"

"I guess if I can handle you, the question would be can you handle me?"

"So can we handle each other?"

"I think we can. It's a big house anyway. It's not like we can't go for separate areas if we really want to. Although, I don't always think that's a good thing."

"Force people together so they can work the problems out?"

"Something like that. That typically works, doesn't it?"

"I think so. For the most part."

His heart felt light, and as he got a rag and started toward the table, he couldn't keep from smiling. He hadn't expected to talk about their relationship, but that conversation had made him happy as well. He didn't exactly feel like they had anything settled between them, but he felt like they both knew what direction they wanted to go, and they were in agreement on it. He also felt like Mallie kind of liked him. Or maybe was starting to really like him. He tucked away the idea that she liked it when he made her laugh. Not that she wanted him to be a silly goofball, but just that she liked humor, and he supposed what person wouldn't rather have someone respond with laughter and a joke than anger and harsh words?

Maybe he would have to talk to the pastor, because he kind of suspected that humor was almost as important as commitment and honesty in a relationship.

He certainly admired it in Mallie. Admired the fact that she had determined that she was going to be content whatever happened.

"How did you feel about the cows? We didn't really get to talk about that either, I mean we talked about getting them, but if I set up an appointment for sometime next week when I get home, are you okay with that?"

"Yeah. I'd be okay with doing it today too, but if anything goes wrong... Kind of like the goat?"

"Yeah. Although, I think that if Ellen is going to sell us a cow that's pregnant, she'd tell us about it."

"True, but at the same time, I think I would rather be safe than sorry on this one."

"I can't disagree with that. I think I'll go ahead and set up a time, and then—"

"Mom!"

"Uncle Jones!"

The conversation was interrupted by the girls bursting through the door and running into the kitchen calling their names.

"We found kittens!"

# Chapter 25

"You haven't seen the mom?" Mallie asked as they stood in the small shed out back, looking at the squirming kittens. The shed was one of the few buildings that had been on the property and hadn't been torn down when Annika bought it.

"There's a dead cat out behind the barn. We saw it this morning. I was going to tell you, but I knew you guys were talking and I didn't want to interrupt you. Then, Bella found these."

The girls had told them that the goat had jumped out of her stall and had run straight toward the shed, kicking it and nosing at the door until they opened it.

Once inside, the goat had gone straight to the kittens, and she was there now, her nose down, sniffing.

"Maybe we should go look at it?" Mallie said, glancing at Jones to see what he said.

Since their chat in the kitchen, where he laughed and joked, but held her close, and seemed like he was interested in more than a platonic relationship, she hadn't quite gotten the butterflies in her stomach under control.

She wasn't sure why that made her nervous, other than she really liked him. The more time she spent with him, the deeper those feelings seemed to get. She had been afraid that it was just her.

They hadn't settled anything for sure, but she felt a lot better about the direction they were heading. Even if she didn't feel completely safe to totally fall for him, she thought, at the very least, he wasn't going to break her heart.

But they had a more immediate problem.

"We probably should, although...the kittens seemed hungry."

"Bella wants to be their mom," Toni said matter-of-factly, her eyes on the goat as she nosed the kittens while they blindly tried to climb out of the small indentation in the straw that lay on the floor.

"She might end up having to be. If their mom is dead."

They walked out of the shed, and the girls led them to where the dead cat was.

Once they walked around behind her, they could see that she'd been struggling to have a fourth kitten and had died before it had been born.

"It might have been too big for her," Jones said seriously.

That's what Mallie thought. And she was sad that they hadn't been able to help her or do anything for her, since they'd had no idea there was a cat on the ranch.

She swallowed. Another day, another death. She wasn't sure whether she enjoyed living on the farm or not. If that was the way every day was going to go... But then she thought, they had three live babies in the barn shed. Why was she focusing on the dead one in front of her?

"All right. I think that probably answers the question we all had. Now...can kittens drink goat milk?"

"I can give Dr. Lark a call."

Mallie nodded and waited while Jones called and had a short conversation with Lark.

"She said go for it. She said that they won't drink much at a time, but they'll drink often. Every two hours or so."

"Can we take turns?" the girls asked.

"Someone's going to have to. She said night and day every two hours. Not for a long time, but a couple of weeks."

"Eventually they'll be able to eat by themselves," Mallie pointed out.

"Yes, it will be a few weeks, and eventually they will."

They stared at the kittens and watched the goat tenderly nuzzle them with her nose.

"It's almost like she thinks she's their mom," Flo said, looking at how the goat gently guided the kittens, trying to keep them in their little nest.

"I think probably because she just lost her babies, she's feeling particularly motherly. But she can hardly adopt them. A goat can't feed kittens."

"Someone's going to have to milk the goat!" Mallie said, fear filling up her chest. She had no idea how to milk an animal.

"Good point. When Lark said that, she said it so matter-of-factly that it didn't even dawn me that one of us was going to have to..." Jones looked at the goat, his face showing his horror, then turned back to Mallie. "...milk her."

"I'll do it!" Toni said, jumping up. She walked over to the goat, then bit her lip. "I'm not sure how though."

"Surely there is a YouTube video for that," Mallie said, and she wasn't really joking.

In fact, she pulled out her phone and typed into the search engine that came up.

"Yeah. There are about a hundred videos on it," she said as the search results populated.

"All right then. I don't think we'll need a whole lot for the kittens, but I guess if we're going to need goat milk, we need to milk the goat the whole way. That's something that Lark said yesterday."

"I remember that. She said if we were going to milk her, we just had to make sure that we did it until she was...empty. That wasn't the word she used."

"Dry. She said milk her until she was dry. Which meant that you couldn't get any more milk out of her."

They looked at each other. Then looked at the goat. Mallie felt a little bit bad for her. She was going to be their guinea pig. After all, no one standing there had ever milked a goat before, and they were going to get their practice on her. Poor thing.

"In every video that I'm seeing, the goat is tied up somehow. I suppose it would be kind of hard to milk her if she were walking around loose."

"Maybe we could feed her. That might help her stand still."

"I guess I could call and see how soon the feed is going to be here. Coleman said he was going to order it for today, and I'm sure he told them that we had nothing. So hopefully they made it a priority."

He pulled his phone out of his pocket and began to call, while Mallie continued to look at the kittens with the girls.

"I wonder if we can touch them?" she said as she knelt down with one finger out.

"Uncle Jones, I think I hear something. Maybe the feed truck is here."

Jones turned around from the front of the shed, and he said, "Good ears. I'm pretty sure that's it."

"Do you want us to give you a hand?" Mallie wasn't sure what exactly it involved when the feed truck came, but she was willing to help if she could.

"It's okay. I want to make sure that Bella stays in here, unless you want to come out. Which is fine. But maybe we'll just keep the goat in here and bring her feed and water in, and maybe somebody can hold her while somebody else tries to milk her."

That sounded like a plan to Mallie, and she and Flo stayed with the kittens while Toni walked out with Jones to see what they needed to do with the feed truck.

"I've never had kittens before. Mom said when we got a farm, we'd be able to get animals. And I was really looking forward to it."

"Your mom loved animals?"

"I don't know. But she always seemed to think that it was important that I got to have animals. She never really said."

Mallie nodded and figured that Annika might not have been an animal person, but she recognized a love for animals in her daughter and wanted to foster that. It must have been hard to juggle such a huge career and a child as well.

Of course, Jones had been a quiet support in her background. It made Mallie wonder if Annika would have been such a huge success without him. He had been content to give her the spotlight while he stood in the shadows.

It made her long to be able to talk to his sister and see if she realized how much he had given for her.

He obviously loved her too. He spoke about her with admiration and love.

"It makes me sad that Mom's not here," Flo said softly, one finger out stroking the white kitten.

One of the other kittens was orange, and one was black. The mama cat had been orange. Interesting that only one of her kittens took after her.

"Sometimes people say that when people are in heaven, they can look down and see what we're doing here on earth. I don't know for sure whether that's true or not. I kinda suspect it isn't. But I know that when you get to heaven, your mom's going to want to hear all about everything that you did. And while she's not here now, she wants you to grow into a beautiful and kind and considerate person. So I hope she always stays close to your mind. And I think it's perfectly natural for you to want her to be here."

She hoped those were correct words. She didn't want to give Flo some kind of hope that her mom was watching her, when she couldn't find any evidence of that in the Bible, other than the verse "with so great a cloud of witnesses," but that didn't necessarily mean that people were sitting in grandstands in heaven watching what was going on on earth. If heaven were truly as what the Bible said, and she believed it was, of course, people who were there wouldn't really care about what was going on on earth. They'd want to have their sights set on all the wonderful things in heaven.

"I guess I'll have a lot of good things to tell her whenever I get there."

"Yeah. She's gonna want to hear all the good things."

"Uncle Jones smiles a lot more since you're here."

"Was he serious before?"

"Before Mom died, he laughed a lot too. But after she died, I guess we both just kind of got sad. And Uncle Jones quit laughing."

"I'm sorry."

"I like that he's laughing again. I like that we are doing fun things. I like that I have animals to pet, and friends to play with, and...can I call Toni my sister?"

"You sure can. I hope eventually we'll love each other and be a family."

Flo didn't say anything for a minute, and then she said, "I already have a mom."

"I know. I was thinking the other day that I wasn't sure whether you would have room in your heart for two moms or not. I... I have room in my heart for two daughters."

She didn't say anything more, and she let Flo chew on that for a little bit.

They sat there in silence for a few minutes until Toni walked in the shed door.

"I have feed. And Mr. Jones said that he would bring some water."

"Okay."

"The feed truck driver said that if you put a rope around her neck, you should be able to hold her if she gets done eating before somebody gets done milking her. And he showed me how you start at the top and you squeeze down." Toni lifted her fingers up and showed her hand squeezing with her first finger then her second finger then her third then her pinky.

"All right. Would you like me to hold her while you try?"

"Can I try on the other side?" Flo asked.

"I don't see why not. I don't know whether she's used to being milked or not. I... I don't know anything about it."

"I guess we'll just figure it out. The feed truck guy said that even if she does kick us, it's not going to hurt. Goats aren't like horses or cows. At least that's what he said, and then he laughed. I wasn't sure exactly what was funny about that, but I thought that meant that we probably don't have to worry about getting hurt. Or at least not too bad."

That wasn't completely reassuring to Mallie, but it made sense.

They got a rope tied around the goat's neck, who didn't seem to mind at all. In fact, Mallie got the idea that she was used to it, and Toni found a small container that would work for her to eat her feed out of. She poured the scoop she had into it.

"The feed truck man said that we need to keep the feed somewhere where the goat can't get it, because if it's anywhere she can climb to or sniff out, she'll get into it. He also laughed when he said that goats are really hard to keep in."

Mallie wasn't sure exactly what they'd gotten themselves into, but from the way Bella was hanging around the kittens, she didn't think they had to worry about her getting out too soon.

"Maybe I should find an eyedropper, and we should try to feed the kittens before it gets too cold."

She tried to think about where she might have an eyedropper. They had just moved everything into the house in the last couple of weeks, and it wasn't too hard to remember that she put some medicine that had an eyedropper dispenser in the top shelf of the cupboard by the stove.

"I'll be right back."

She stood up, gave her legs a minute to get used to the change in position, then ran into the house, grabbing the eyedropper before she came back out.

It took a little bit for the girls to get used to the motion that it took to milk the goat, but by the time they practiced for five minutes or so, both of them were having, if not a steady stream of milk, a somewhat decent stream.

Mallie had brought back a clean cup when she came out, and once the girls were good at getting milk out, they filled it up half full for her. She knew she wouldn't use even a tiny bit of that amount, but that much would keep it warm, versus having just a small amount.

She was able to get a little bit of milk into each one of the kittens, with the white kitten being the smallest and the weakest.

She had no idea whether they would be able to keep them alive or not, but she glanced at her watch and then put the time in her notes app.

She had each of the girls set an alarm for two hours from then, and she set her own as well.

"I think we'll need to take turns. If each of us takes one shift, then especially at night, we'll be able to have six solid hours of sleep. Which is better than getting up every two hours."

"But we can get up if we want to, can't we?" Toni asked, concerned that she might miss something.

"I suppose you can, but you might feel better if you get your rest at night and then watch every feeding during the day."

She didn't want to forbid her daughter from getting up every two hours if she wanted to, but she probably didn't understand how tired that was going to make her.

"The other danger is that you'll be getting up when it's not your turn, and then when it is your turn, you'll be too tired to get up, and the kittens will miss their meal."

Toni's eyes got big, and her mouth formed an O. She didn't want to be the reason that the kittens didn't eat, and she understood immediately that it would be better to sleep through a couple of feedings than to miss the one that she was supposed to give.

"Okay, but I don't have to miss any of the feedings until tonight, right?"

"Exactly. We'll just make sure that we feed them every two hours, and whoever shows up can show up."

"Should we milk the goat every two hours?"

Mallie bit her lip. They hadn't gotten much milk out of the goat, but it wouldn't take much to feed the kittens.

"Let's do that. I'm not sure how often baby goats eat, but it's probably pretty close to every two hours. I don't think it will hurt her. And it's not like she's giving a lot of milk anyway."

"What about the middle of the night? Should we come out and feed the goat and milk her and feed the kittens?"

"How about I take this much milk inside. With as little the kittens ate, this will be plenty to last all night. The rest of the milk that we get today, we'll feed right away. And...maybe we should save some, just in case she stops giving it."

She wasn't sure, with the poor condition that the goat was in, whether she would continue to produce milk or not. She thought Lark had said or maybe it was Coleman that she might not produce milk at all, so they probably should be grateful that they had enough to feed the kittens.

"What will we do if she quits giving milk?" Florence asked, her eyes filled with worry.

"Well, we probably ought not to worry about things that are not likely to happen." Mallie laughed. "Maybe we shouldn't worry about things that are likely to happen either. After all, God says that He's going to take care of us. But I think there is such a thing as kitten formula, and maybe we can check that out, either in town or online."

Her words reassured the girls, and the worry lines disappeared from between Flo's eyes.

There was a part of Mallie that wanted to worry. Worry that the kittens were going to die, and the girls were going to see yet another death on the farm. She didn't want them to have to go through that, but she also knew that just like the baby kids, just like the mama cat, death was a part of life. And as much as she would like to protect her daughters from it, she also knew that it was good for them to go through it. Even though it was hard.

*Lord, if we can have a little reprieve from the death and let these babies live, I would appreciate it.*

She didn't say that out loud. She didn't want the girls to even consider that she wasn't completely sure the kittens were going to make it. She was supposed to be confident, the adult in the picture.

"How are things going?" Jones asked as he popped his head in the shed door.

A truck motor fading off into the distance indicated the feed truck had left.

"All three of the kittens ate, and we all set alarms on our phones to ring in two hours."

"Great. Buzz said that the goat shouldn't be too hard to milk, and he also said if she kicked, it wasn't going to hurt."

"I don't think she kicked at all, did she, girls?"

"You mean you milked her already?" Jones asked, surprise in his voice.

"They sure did. They did a great job. Look at all this milk," Mallie said, holding up the half full cup of milk that she had.

"Is that all she gave?"

"She gave a little bit more, but not much."

"Buzz said that they sell milk replacer for kittens at the feed store. Maybe we should invest in some."

"I actually just told the girls that that might be a good idea. Although, with all the kittens ate, this is enough milk for a really long time."

"Is somebody going to get up and feed them tonight?" Jones asked, stepping in the shed and kneeling down to get a better look at the kittens before reaching out and scratching Bella's face.

"I think we have it organized, but if you want to take a turn, I'm sure everyone will let you."

"Maybe I'd better watch first and see how it's done."

"I'm not entirely sure I did it right. But you're certainly welcome to watch me if you want to."

"Aren't there YouTube videos for that?" Jones asked with a smile.

"Maybe I'll have to make one. I'm almost a professional. I feel like I need to put my own video up."

"Pass it along, right?"

They laughed together and looked at the goat and the kittens for a bit more.

"Do you think that it would be okay to leave the goat in here with them?"

"I guess. I don't think she'll hurt them. She seems to just want to nuzzle them and be close to them."

"You don't think she'll lie on them?"

"I don't know."

They thought about it for a little bit, and then Flo said, "I think she deserves to stand here with the kittens. She's feeding them, even if they're not getting the milk directly from her, and she obviously loves them."

They were interrupted by a moo outside the door.

"What's that?" Mallie asked, jerking her head toward the outside.

"I forgot to tell you. Somehow Billy showed up here today. It was weird, I went out to the feed truck, and there he was. The feed truck guy was surprised too. It's kind of like he's following me around. Since he practically chased me down the sidewalk since I first arrived in Sweet Water."

"Rumor around town has it that Billy was in love with Munchy, the pig. Maybe he's decided he's in love with you instead," Toni said, laughing.

"Well, he's wasting his time. And someone can tell him that. I would, but he shakes those horns at me and all I want to do is run away."

"Billy is as gentle as a lamb," Toni said, and she almost rolled her eyes, except there was a knock on the shed door, and they looked to see Billy was shaking his head outside the shed door hitting his horns against the wood.

"I don't know. It kinda of looks like he's trying to knock the door down."

"We can't really let him in here, not unless we move the kittens."

"That would be a good idea. That way we don't have to worry about whether or not the goat's gonna lie down on them. We can put them in that manger over there," Jones said after looking around the shed. "I don't think they're big enough to fall out, and that way if the goat wants to nuzzle them, she can, and she can lie down right below them."

"And Billy can be in if he wants to be?" Toni asked, looking out the crack at Billy who bawled again.

"I think he might just be hungry, but I'm fine if we put him in. I don't think he'll hurt the kittens either. Cows are not exactly known for being aggressive toward anything," Jones said. "Except me," he added quickly, causing all the ladies around him to laugh.

"I'm glad Jonna brought her Pork Colorado. My breakfast has almost worn off, and I'm starting to get hungry." Mallie looked at her phone. "I can't believe what time it is."

"It's been a pretty busy day."

He spent a few more minutes arranging the kittens in the manger, making sure the goat had water where she couldn't spill it, and letting Billy in the pen with her.

Billy went straight over to the goat, mooing softly, like he had found his long-lost love.

"I sure hope Munchy doesn't hear about this. She's liable to be jealous," Toni muttered.

"Yeah. I'm a little bit disappointed. He's not very loyal."

"Maybe Munchy found another man, and Billy is just trying to soothe his heartbreak with a rebound relationship," Mallie suggested, feeling bad that everyone seemed to assume that everything was all Billy's fault. She patted him on the back. "Right, Billy?"

"Glad someone's defending the man in that relationship." Jones grinned.

They laughed, leaving the shed together, with Jones taking her hand as they walked across the yard.

She looked up at him, and he smiled down, and she remembered the words that she had said earlier, about how she liked it. That knowledge seemed to be in Jones's eyes as he grinned at her.

They went in and got the Pork Colorado ready, which was very easy to do. All they had to do was break it up in the crockpot and get the containers of toppings out that Jonna had provided.

It turned out to be a delicious meal and a great ending to their day.

As they gathered around the front porch, the girls sitting in rocking chairs and Jones and she on the swing, dusk fell and they sang softly together.

Mallie, feeling content down to her toes, dreaded the next day, since Jones was leaving.

It made her sad and made her long for... She wasn't sure what.

She knew she'd miss this, miss having him there beside her, miss knowing that if something happened, she wasn't going to have to face it alone.

It's funny how easy it had been to get used to having him around.

She would have said she was a confirmed single mom, but she hadn't realized how much she missed having a partner.

She had told him whatever he decided she would be fine with and she would adjust to, and she knew that that was true. But she found herself praying that he would decide that he wanted to stay home. That's where she wanted him.

# Chapter 26

"Good night, girls," Jones said as Florence and Toni went into bed. They had just finished feeding kittens, and Toni was going to take the first turn at feeding them at midnight. So they were both going to try to get some sleep.

He was kind of happy about that. He loved both girls and wanted to be a good father, but he also appreciated having some time alone with Mallie.

Ever since they talked in the morning, and if he were honest, even before that, he had longed to get to know her better.

Or maybe just to sit and be near her. As near to her as he could get. The longer time went on, the more he dreaded having to leave the next day. If this was how he was going to feel every time he had to leave, he didn't think he was going to be able to do it.

Well, he knew he would be able to, because a man had to do what a man had to do, but he was going to hate it. And considering that he didn't have to work, didn't have to go sing, didn't have to tour, he figured that he probably wouldn't.

There would be people who would be let down by his decision. People who would need to find another job, and he hated that. He hated the idea that they couldn't depend on him. He wanted them to be able to, but he also knew that he had to make the decision that was best for his family, not necessarily the one that was best for everyone else. Because, sometimes the two just didn't match up.

"What are you thinking about?" Mallie asked.

"I think when women ask that, it's a trick question," he said, laughing a little.

She waited.

"I don't want to leave. And I was thinking about the people who depend on me, depend on me singing in order to make a living. I...don't want to let people down, but I also am leaning strongly toward staying home. Whatever we can do here, if anything, is what we'll do. I... I don't think I can face trips like this on a weekly basis."

Mallie let out a breath. "Maybe I shouldn't say this, but that's what I want. I've been dreading you leaving too. I told you earlier that I just couldn't believe how, after being comfortable being alone for so long, I have really gotten used to you being around and hate the idea of you going."

"Yeah. I'm a nice fella to have around."

She chuckled, and they sat quietly for a little bit.

"Thanks for helping us with the kittens and the goat and everything today," she said.

"Of course. It was fun. Except for that steer. He has a thing for me. It's really weird."

"I don't think it's you. I actually thought that he really seemed taken with the goat. But it must have been love at first sight, because as far as I know, Billy hadn't seen her before."

"You know, there could be such a thing as love at first sight. I didn't really used to believe in that, but... We haven't been together very long, and... I guess I don't know if I would term it love, but I definitely feel attached to you, in a way that I'm not even sure I can explain."

"I don't think it was love at first sight."

"Love at first sound. Because I heard you sing before I saw your face."

"Now I think you're being charming. Or maybe that's flattering."

"It's sincere, whatever it is."

"I love singing with you. I love listening to you sing. It...just sounds right. Which is a weird way to put it, but it's true."

"Are you sure you guys are going to be okay by yourselves here?" he asked, and although he wanted to continue that line of talking, he wasn't sure how he felt, and it made him a little uncomfortable. He didn't want to make any promises he couldn't keep, any declarations that weren't true. And he felt it was a little bit early to tell her that he loved her. After all, he barely knew her. But that's what he wanted to say. So, he just needed to change the subject.

"I think we'll be fine. It wasn't hard to milk the goat. She stood still every time. The girls are going to be milking her overnight, and feeding the kittens wasn't hard either. So I guess unless we have another catastrophe somewhere, we'll be fine."

"The contractor should be in. He said he was going to have some parts, something about the water and electric in the basement. I forget exactly what he did say, because I was on the phone with him and there were so many other things going on that I was really only half paying attention."

"Understandable. And most things are working well anyway. It was just the wiring for the basement bathroom or something, wasn't it?"

"Yeah. The one that if we have people coming into the studio, they'll be using that. It was kind of a last-minute addition, since I figured you weren't going to want people upstairs traipsing through the house if it wasn't necessary."

"I don't mind, but I guess it will be nice if we ever have children." Her words broke off short. She obviously hadn't meant to say that.

"So you want kids?" he asked casually, trying to sound natural. Of course they were going to have to talk about children. But he really hadn't thought about them himself.

"I... I guess I hadn't really thought about it. Except, maybe I had, because I haven't really even been thinking about it but those words just came out."

"I kinda thought that's what happened, when you broke off so quickly."

"I'm sorry. I didn't mean to make things awkward."

"Not awkward. I love the girls we have, but I guess I wouldn't mind having children. I can't say it was ever something I dreamed about, but…" He let his words trail off, because it was true, up until this point in his life, he never thought about having children, but there was something about Mallie that brought that desire out in him. He didn't think it was his biological clock ticking. Did men have biological clocks? He wasn't sure. But he could see himself having children with Mallie. Which wasn't terribly scary, and maybe it should be.

"What?" she prompted, and he realized he had totally forgotten what he was saying.

"But I guess with you I kind of want them." He huffed out a laugh. "You really turned my life upside down. You have no idea how much you've shifted my brain until I don't even really recognize myself."

"Really? Is that a bad thing?" She sounded concerned.

"No. I think that you've turned me and I'm thinking less about myself and more about others. Actually I kind of like the direction I'm going, and I like that it was your influence. After all, you want to be around people who make you a better person, right?"

"Absolutely. Anyone who helps you be closer to the Lord is someone that you want to spend time with."

"And here I am, blessed enough to be married to that person. I kind of feel like God was smiling at me, and I didn't even realize it until just now."

"He was smiling at us both."

He had his arm on the swing behind her, but he allowed it to drop, and he pulled her closer.

She came willingly, her hand settling on his leg.

He wished he didn't have his trip looming up in front of him. Wished that they just had the rest of their lives stretching out together, with only short separations or none.

"If you like, once I leave, and I come back, I never want to leave again. That sounds like something a ten-year-old would say, doesn't it?"

"Or a teenager. But it's kind of funny how much like a teenager I feel. I just kinda feel a little giddy sometimes. Is that crazy?"

"I don't think so. But what do I know?"

"Yeah, I've been thinking about singing together as a family. I like that idea more and more. It's like the more we do together, the stronger our family will be. I just don't want the girls to see it as work and come to hate it."

"I agree. But they actually gravitate toward us when we sing. So I feel like they're going to enjoy it. As long as it doesn't become one long practice session after another, or maybe making them do things that are too hard for them."

"Yeah. I was thinking that it would be fun for everyone to learn an instrument, but I didn't want to suggest that and push it. But I feel like they'll enjoy doing it if it's their own idea."

"Do you play?"

"No, but I do read music. I took piano lessons when I was a kid, but I never practiced, and the only thing that I remember is where middle C is and how to read music."

"Then they weren't a total waste."

"No. Although my mom might have disagreed with you."

"Where is your family?" he asked, realizing he didn't even know that much about her.

"My parents split when I was younger. I went with my dad, and Mom really kind of lost track of me. She passed away of pancreatic cancer a few years ago. I visited her a couple of times at the end, and she regretted not having a better relationship with me, at least that's what she said. But at that point, it was too late."

"That's sad."

"I know. I guess that's what I thought when she said that, and I decided I didn't want to do that. I don't want to find that I put other things ahead of my family, didn't have a relationship with my children, and now it's too late. You know?"

"Yeah. Maybe that's part of the reason I really think that I don't want to tour. Family has to be the most important thing."

He appreciated that they agreed on that, although his heart bled at the fact that Mallie didn't have a mother who loved her. Or at least, she didn't feel loved.

They sat for a while, before the chill got to them, and they went in, saying a quiet good night as they went to their separate rooms.

The decision that he thought was going to be so hard solidified in his mind, and it felt exactly right. If they couldn't make music together at home, he would find something else to do.

# Chapter 27

Jones didn't leave until after lunch, and it felt like the entire afternoon stretched before them, long and hard and lonely.

Mallie wanted to roll her eyes at herself, just because she was acting like a lovesick teenager, but she couldn't help it. She didn't want him to go, and it was all she could do to stand there and smile and not beg him to stay. Which was ridiculous.

They had just fed the kittens, with Bella and Billy still in the shed together. Billy did seem to have an attachment to the goat, and the goat definitely had an attachment to the kittens. Mallie wouldn't go so far as to say the goat thought she was the kittens' mother, but she definitely didn't want to leave them and stayed right beside them.

It probably helped that she had her feed and water in there, and she seemed to be eating and drinking okay, which is what Lark told them to watch for.

Of course, Billy ate the lion's share of the hay, although they didn't let him have any of the goat's feed.

Putting an arm around each girl, as they stood there facing the direction where Jones's truck had disappeared, she said, "Let's go into the house and decide what we're going to have for supper."

She couldn't think of anything else to do. Although, surely there were other things. They could work on their garden or decide where they wanted to put a swimming pool. Jones had said he had rented a backhoe that was supposed to be there the day after he got home from his trip. They'd discussed a few places and considered putting in a small building beside it, like a changing room with a shower.

It seemed so rich compared to what she was used to, but she couldn't deny that she was enjoying life on the farm.

Except, it stunk that she would be alone for the next five days.

They met the contractor on the front walk.

He burst out of the door at not quite a sprint but screeched to a stop when he saw them.

"I'm sorry. I just found out my wife and son were in an accident. I don't think they're seriously injured, but I need to go to them. I'll finish up later."

That's all he said before he ran off again.

Mallie nodded and called after him, "Go on. Take care of your family,"

He threw a hand up in acknowledgment and continued to run.

Mallie said a silent prayer that the contractor's family would be okay. And she made a note to ask Jones about it if she didn't see the contractor before he did.

They didn't need the bathroom in the basement, and if it took him a week or two to get back, it would be fine.

It was a little overcast, and she felt like it might rain, but she hadn't seen the weather. Still, when they walked in the house, it felt dark, and she reached to switch the lights on.

There was nothing.

"I wonder..." She walked to the kitchen, switching the lights on there. Nothing again. "The contractor must have forgotten to turn the electricity on before he left."

"That's okay. We can live without electricity."

"Sure. We can have a campfire tonight," Toni said cheerfully.

Oh, to be young again and to not care about creature comforts like electricity.

Mallie laughed and realized the girls were right. It was summer, they didn't need the heat, and the days hadn't been hot enough to even think about running the air conditioner.

They didn't need electricity.

But when she walked over to the sink to wash her hands and the water didn't come out, she realized that maybe they had a bigger problem than what she thought.

"I think he forgot to turn the water back on too."

This time, there was some concern in her voice. Even if he had turned it back on, she realized they would need electricity to run the pump.

They could live without electricity. And they could probably survive without water, but...she really didn't want to.

Maybe for a day, but not for five, until Jones came back.

She looked at her phone. Jones was in the air. His plane was supposed to touch down within the next hour. He promised to text her when he landed safely.

"Well, girls, let's go downstairs and see if we can figure this out. If not, when Jones texts me that he landed safely, I'll ask him if he knows how to turn the water on. I don't want to worry him, so I might not mention that we don't have electricity."

"He's going to want to know. Even if he can't do anything about it, he can pray for us."

Mallie stopped with her hand on the cellar doorknob and turned to look at Florence. "You're right. That's a good point. And I guess I don't really want to keep it from him anyway. Even though I don't want him to worry about us."

"No, but if it were you, you'd want to know," Toni pointed out reasonably.

She couldn't help it, the girls were right, and she knew it. "I can't argue with that. So, I'll let him know. But I'm also going to let him know that we have everything under control. Because we do, right?"

"Yeah. Maybe we can sleep in the tents tonight. Not that it matters, but since there are no lights anyway, we might as well sleep outside."

"Good idea. We'd better conserve the batteries on our phones too. Because if we can't plug them in to charge them, we'll want them to last as long as possible. So... Maybe we'll just use one at a time?"

"That's fine with me. We can set ours down somewhere, and we'll use the alarm on yours for the kittens until the battery goes dead, and then we'll use mine, and then Flo's. And then, if we need more battery, I guess we'll have to go in to the diner and eat. We can plug them in there."

"Of course. Or we could go to the community center for a bit. And anyone in town would let us take showers if we need them. Although, we'll have to make sure we have plenty of water for Bella and Billy."

"I just filled their buckets up before we came in. And the water trough is full," Florence said.

"Then it looks like we're well taken care of."

Mallie wasn't worried; everything would be fine.

They got hot dogs out of the refrigerator, and an onion, and took some rolls and went out to build a small fire.

"I don't want to make it too big, because it's a little bit windy. So once we finish, we want to make sure we put it out."

They didn't have water to put it out, but she didn't say that. They ate quickly, then put the fire out, and just sat for a bit before Flo said, "How about we put up the tents?"

They were going to do it yesterday, but they got sidetracked with all the animals, and by the time they were done, they were all too tired.

So, they went down to the basement, found where Jones had said the tents were, and took them both out.

As they started setting the bigger tent up, her phone buzzed with a text.

**I landed safely. Everything good there?**

"He made it okay, girls," Mallie said.

Then she texted back.

**The contractor had a family emergency and I think he forgot to turn the water and electricity back on before he left. We're fine. We ate hot dogs over a campfire and now are setting up the tents. I probably shouldn't text much because I want to try to save the battery on my phone.**

His text came back immediately.

**Coming home.**

She smiled. That made her feel good that he was that concerned about her, but he really didn't need to waste his trip.

**We're fine. I promise.**

**I'll see if I can find a flight.**

**I'm not trying to talk you out of coming home. Because I would love it if you did, but I promise, we're fine.**

**I knew I shouldn't have left. I didn't want to. Let me see what I can find.**

**Okay.**

She ended up sending that last text, because she didn't want to argue anymore. He was going to come home, she wasn't going to complain about it, and she had let him know that they were going to truly be fine.

"He said he was going to see if he could find a flight home."

"Really?" Flo smiled and couldn't keep the excitement out of her eyes. "I didn't want to complain, but it's been lonely here without Uncle Jones."

"I felt the same way," Mallie said sheepishly.

"It did seem kinda quiet, and when the lights went out, I knew if he were here, he would figure out a way to fix it. But I didn't want to say that, because I didn't want to make you feel bad, Mom. I knew you were doing your best."

"Yeah. That was nice of you to consider my feelings."

She didn't mind, because it was true. She was terrible with fixing stuff. She supposed she could look up online and see if there were any videos that would show how to turn the water on and off in the house, but she wasn't sure she wanted to mess with it. Knowing her luck, she probably would break something else rather than fix the problem at hand, and it wasn't a dire emergency. If they ran out of water, that might be a different story, but there were plenty of neighbors she could talk to if she needed to. She just didn't want to bother anyone because she didn't need anything right away.

They worked for a while and were able to get the first tent up. It was big enough to sleep both girls with room to spare.

"Can we see if we can get Bella to stay with us?" Florence asked.

"And the kittens. If we can get the kittens to stay, then when we wake up in the middle of the night, we won't have to go anywhere."

"Well," Mallie said, part of her wishing that Jones was there to help her make the decision. "I think it will be okay. I just think it might be a good idea to put the kittens in a box or something so that no one rolls all over on them or steps on them in the middle of the night."

"Okay!" the girls said.

"Are you going to put your tent up?"

Mallie looked at it, considering. She had zero desire to sleep outside in the tent, but she also wasn't completely comfortable letting the girls sleep outside by themselves, especially since Jones wasn't there. Maybe if they had done it before he left, she would be more comfortable.

"I think I will put mine up."

"We can give you a hand after we go get Bella and the babies."

"What are you going to do if Billy wants to sleep with you guys too?"

"He has to stay out. His horns will rip a hole in the tent," Toni said, and she had zero compassion for poor Billy staying outside.

Mallie had to smile. Poor Billy, he didn't realize that he was going to be relegated to observer status.

Of course, he probably wouldn't mind. As long as they left a little hole open, so he could put his nose in and smell that they were still there.

By the time it got dark, her tent was up, and they had gotten sleeping bags from the basement, as well as a box for the kittens who were snug inside the larger tent, along with Bella.

As Mallie suspected, Billy wanted to be in the tent too, but he seemed to understand that it wasn't big enough for him, and he stood right outside the opening, his nose pushed inside.

At least he didn't try to get the rest of his body in.

She hadn't heard anything more from Jones, and she was tempted to text him, but she didn't. She really did want to try to save the battery on her phone, and she assumed that if he would have found a flight home, he would have said so.

She was a little disappointed but not upset. He probably had his mind on all the things that he needed to accomplish, and maybe he, like her, was hoping he could get everything done that needed to be done so he wouldn't have to make another trip.

She fell asleep, thinking that there were only four more days until he came home.

# Chapter 28

J ones hadn't had time to text Mallie. He checked at the nearest airline counter, and the next flight was getting ready to board. He bought a ticket immediately, figured his luggage was never going to make it, and decided that he would try to find it some other time.

Running for the gate, he barely made it before they closed the doors.

Pulling his phone out, he texted Sebastian, letting him know what happened.

Sebastian called him immediately.

Jones didn't want to talk, but he knew that he owed Sebastian an explanation. After all, his livelihood depended in part on Jones, and Jones felt bad that he was letting his friend down.

They worked together, true, but he considered Sebastian a friend.

Although they were definitely not in agreement over his decision, Sebastian understood about the importance of family, and he couldn't give Jones a hard time.

"I wish you would reconsider. I've been sending out feelers, and the industry is excited about a Jones Dunn solo act. Especially considering that you might have Annika's daughter with you. That would pull the heartstrings of every single one of her fans, and you would have a built-in following. Are you sure you won't reconsider?"

"I'm sure. I spent the last week and a half thinking about it, and…I might do something at home. We have that recording studio thanks to Annika, or maybe I'll just be a farmer."

Sebastian snorted. "You're hardly cut out for farming. What are you gonna do, sit on a stool and play your guitar to your cows?"

"Maybe. I've heard they grow better if they have good music."

"Good music, that's subjective. Possibly, cows might think that they would rather hear you on a CD than acoustic in the field."

"Very funny. And not convincing at all. Hey, they're telling us we have to shut our phones off. I need to go."

He hung up and started writing a text to his wife, when the lady beside him said, "They said to shut your phones off. You could mess everything up. We could crash. Did you hear about the accident on the runway where a hundred people died? My best friend told me it was because someone was on their phone and refused to shut it off!"

"I just need to let my wife know—"

"Do you want to get home safely to her? Then shut the thing off."

He looked up to see the stewardess looking at him.

He didn't want to cause a brawl on the plane, so he apologized, smiled at the lady beside him, and shoved his phone in his brief-case.

He'd text her when he landed. Except, it would be late. He wouldn't want to wake her up.

And he was right, as he pulled into the drive it was after two. Although, it wasn't so late and he wasn't so tired that he didn't notice there were two tents in the yard.

He smiled. They had never gotten the tents out yesterday, and his girls must have talked Mallie into putting them up last night. He laughed; if they didn't have any electricity and water, they might as well be sleeping in a tent.

One was a little bit bigger than the other, and he guessed that Mallie was in the smaller one.

He also guessed that the girls were in theirs with the goat, since he could see that Billy stood outside of the larger tent.

Just to be sure, he used a small flashlight to shine in the tent door, and sure enough, his wife lay in the tent alone, sound asleep.

He shut his light out quickly so he didn't wake her up, wondering what to do.

Finally, he toed his boots off, set them right inside the tent door, and ducked in.

"Mallie?" he said, low and soft. He did not touch her. He hoped she recognized his voice. "Mallie, it's Jones."

"Jones?" she asked, her voice heavy with sleep. "You came back?" She sounded happy. Even if she still sounded sleepy.

"Yeah. I couldn't leave you guys here without water and electricity."

"I told you we were fine."

"I wanted to be here."

"I want you here," she admitted.

"I just wanted you to know I was home."

"Come on. You can lie down. There's not a whole lot of room in my sleeping bag, but I think I can find enough to share with you. Unless... You're too old to sleep inside a tent in a sleeping bag?"

"Oh, lady. That was low."

She chuckled softly, and he smiled as he felt around in the darkness. Going around behind her as she moved over and he slipped into her sleeping bag.

"Actually, I just came home because I thought you were going to let me share your sleeping bag. And I wasn't going to miss out on an opportunity like that."

"You didn't even know we were putting the tents up."

"I know. I was just kidding. But if I had known, I would have urged the pilot to go faster."

He put an arm around her, tucking his hand underneath her stomach, and she adjusted her head until his arm was underneath it and she lay pressed against him.

"This is just about perfect," he murmured.

"Yeah. Much better than it had been before."

It felt like she fit perfectly against him.

"Did you talk to Sebastian?" she asked in the darkness.

"I did. I told him that I wasn't going to make it, because I had to go back home. I also told him that it looked like I was going to be working from home. I know he'll have his wheels turning and have some ideas for us. Once we get together, hopefully here, we can make some plans. But I think we'll just set up some social media channels, and pages, and everything we can and just try to get the word out. I know he's disappointed, but he understands that I needed to make the decision that was best for my family."

"I appreciate that."

"It wasn't a hardship. It was what I wanted."

He could hear her smiling in the darkness.

"As I was driving away, I regretted one thing."

"Yeah?"

"I should have told you that I loved you before I left. I kept thinking that if anything happened, either to me or to you, I didn't want to leave without you hearing it. So, I said to myself that the first thing I was going to do when I got back was to make sure you knew it. I love you." He paused for a moment. "I think that's why it was so hard for me to leave. It was like I was leaving my heart here. I know that is sappy, but it's the truth. I... I don't want to do that again."

"That's funny. Because it felt like you were taking my heart with you. I love you too."

She rolled so she was on her back, and he leaned up on his elbow, peering down into her face, although he couldn't see anything but shadows in the darkness.

Her hand came up and touched the back of his neck, sending shivers down his spine.

"I regretted something else," she whispered.

"Yeah?"

"I wish I would have asked you to kiss me. I... I thought the same thing. Something could happen, to you, to me, anything. And maybe it was the contractor running out of the house saying that his wife and son had been in an accident. I don't know. I just... I had wanted you to for a while, and I wish that I had asked you before you left."

"Well, I guess I'll have to make up for that."

"I guess you will." They chuckled together.

"Would you be quiet over there? We're trying to sleep." Toni's voice, sleepy and irritated, cut through the darkness.

"Sorry. Just kissing your mother. That's all."

"It sounds like you guys are giggling," Flo said, and her voice was just as irritated and sleepy.

"Isn't it time for you guys to feed the kittens?" Mallie asked, just to get their minds off their irritation.

"Yeah. I guess it is. The alarm should go off in—" She didn't finish her words before the alarm sounded.

And there was rustling in the other tent.

"I think this might be a good time for me to steal a kiss. While they're busy with something else," Jones said in that soft husky tone that sent shivers down her spine, but there was also humor in his voice.

"You're not stealing it if I give it to you."

"Good point."

They were smiling when their lips met, and their teeth clacked together before their heads adjusted and their lips settled firmly on each other.

Mallie ran her hands down his back, and he wished they weren't in a tent beside the girls, because it didn't feel like nearly enough, but he didn't think about that too much more as she sighed, and he threaded his hands through her hair, his heart beating hard and his whole body tingling to his toes.

"I don't know if I want to sleep in a tent tonight," he finally said when he lifted his head.

"Yeah. The walls are pretty thin."

They smiled together, and then she kissed his chin before she turned back on her side, putting her back against his front, and he lay back down, pulling her close.

He supposed they'd have the rest of their lives to spend kissing if they wanted to, although he was definitely tempted to insist that they needed to go in.

But there was something sweet and beautiful just lying next to her, and he fell asleep thinking about how perfectly she fit with him.

He woke up rather rudely, when water dripped on his face.

He could hear pounding on the tent and was surprised it hadn't woken him up before that.

Maybe the rain just started.

"Rats. I totally forgot this tent had a leak."

"Oh. Is that what that is? I was dreaming I was swimming in the ocean." Mallie scrambled up, moving away from the leak.

"It has two leaks, just for your information," she said, moving again.

"I guess we get to go inside after all," he said.

She laughed. "You were thinking you wanted to go inside earlier?"

"I was."

"Me too. Do you think the girls are okay?"

"As far as I know, that tent doesn't leak at all. And this feels like one of those showers that are going to be over before it starts. But all of our stuff is wet."

She laughed. "And who wants to sleep on wet things?" she asked, like that would be the worst thing she could imagine.

"Certainly not me," he said, although he was sure that they could find a dry spot and be just fine.

"All right then, your room or mine?" she asked as she grabbed his hand and tugged him toward the tent flap.

"You choose," he said, smiling to himself.

"All right. Yours," she said, just before she yanked the tent flap open and ran out into the darkness, dragging him with her.

He grinned. He didn't have a problem following her.

# Chapter 29

"**M**om?"

Mallie stirred. Something heavy was lying on top of her. She tried to pull her brain up from the deep sleep she had fallen in and wondered why her back was so toasty warm, but there was something heavy on her, until she realized.

*Jones.*

They had gone into the house in the middle of the night after the rain had started and the tent had leaked.

Now, she was lying in his bed, and he was the warm thing behind her, and his arm was the heavy thing over top of her.

"Mom?"

And that was her daughter.

"Toni?" she said, trying to sound cheerful and wide-awake and totally casual at the same time and feeling like she probably failed miserably.

"Mom? What are you doing?"

"What do you mean what am I doing? I'm sleeping. Or I was, anyway."

Jones stirred behind her, pulling her closer to him and throwing his leg over hers.

She suspected he wasn't quite awake.

"It's a good thing we were out with the kittens. You missed your turn."

"Oh. My shift was six o'clock. And I totally forgot."

"Yeah. You did."

The night before, they'd agreed that since the girls were in the tent with the kittens, they would take turns doing the overnight shifts, and she would take the morning shift at six AM.

"I'm sorry. I totally forgot. Our tent leaked—"

"I know. I looked in this morning and saw that everything was wet. It really leaked!"

"Yeah. And anyway, Jones came home last night."

"Mom. I have eyes. I can see that."

"Of course. Just, I'm not quite awake."

"Anyway. I took care of them, so you can keep sleeping, but I wanted you to know."

So she woke her up just to tell her that she didn't have to get up. She was going to have a little chat with her daughter later, but in the meantime, she said, "Thank you. You want me to do the eight o'clock?"

"No. I'll probably be up. And the kittens are still in the tent anyway. Our tent didn't leak, and I actually really like sleeping in it. I think Flo did too, and we want to sleep there again tonight if we can."

"That's fine with me."

As long as she didn't have to do it. Although, since they still didn't have electricity and water, she might really need a shower.

"All right. I just wanted you to know," Toni said before she turned around and closed the door behind her.

"She seemed like it was the most natural thing in the world to have me here with you. I thought for sure when I heard a voice that we were going to have a lot of explaining to do." Jones's voice rumbled behind her, and his lips grazed her ear.

She shivered. "Me too. I can't believe how blasé she was."

"I hope Flo takes it just as well."

"Me too."

"I don't see why she wouldn't. She and Annika were always trying to hook me up. But... I was saving myself."

Mallie had to laugh outright at that. And she turned until she was facing him, one of her legs sliding over top of his and her hand moving down the smooth skin of his side until it rested on his hip bone.

"Is that so?"

"Sure is. But my wait is over."

She shook her head at his teasing, but then she stopped laughing as his lips grazed her temple, and his hands slid down her waist, and his leg rubbed against hers.

"It sounded to me like we had until eight o'clock before they'd be up again."

"That's what it sounded like to me too," she said, her voice sounding a little shivery.

"I wonder what we can do in the meantime?"

"I have no idea. I guess you can go back to sleep," she said as her lips touched the stubble on his chin and her hand went up to his cheek.

"I guess you could do that. But I don't know, seems like we might be able to figure something else out."

"We could probably go down to the cellar and see if you can figure out how to turn the electricity back on, and the water as well."

"Yeah. That probably ought to be done, but...I don't know. Maybe we ought to exercise before we do that."

"Exercise?" she asked, stifling a giggle.

He grinned. "I guess I'll have to show you, because you sound confused."

"Surely we can think of something else to do. I mean, unless you have some kind of newfangled exercise that I haven't heard of yet."

"That's exactly what I was thinking of. Some kind of newfangled exercise that the rest of the world hasn't caught on to yet. Maybe, instead of starting a family singing channel, you and I can start an exercise channel."

"I think this ought to be a personal channel."

It was a while before they made it down to the basement, and Mallie had to admit that she smiled the whole time.

Enjoy this preview of *Just a Cowboy's Lifetime Love,* just for you!

# Just a Cowboy's Lifetime Love
## Chapter 1

"**I**'m sorry for your loss."

Annie Brooks nodded her head, returned the small, perfunctory hug, and swallowed hard.

She had a funeral to get through, and this wasn't the first time, far from it, and would definitely not be the last time those words had been uttered to her that day.

Sunlight glittered down through the fluorescent green of the new maple leaves.

It was her favorite time of year. Late spring tulips bloomed, waving their bright pink and yellow colors, and irises, purple and white, looking stark against their darker green pointed leaves, were planted in clumps all around the large church property.

It wasn't her regular church. She didn't feel at home here. But, when planning the funeral, she knew they needed to have a place where they could handle the large inflow of people who would be attending.

She had never seen so many people at a church before.

The parking lot was full, and Ty Henderson was directing traffic to park in the field beside the church. They'd gotten permission from the farmer just in case, and Annie was glad someone had had the foresight to do so.

Cars were backed up on the highway waiting to turn in. They would never all be parked in time for the start of the funeral.

It took her a while to realize that they could delay the start. She was in charge. Technically. She could say she didn't want anything to start until every last car was parked and every last person seated.

The idea gave her something to focus on. Something other than the fact that the funeral she could delay was her husband's.

"I'm sorry for your loss."

Another perfunctory hug, another person with sad eyes, compassion oozing from every pore, squeezed her, then walked away, not knowing what else to say.

She wouldn't know what to say to someone in her position. She honestly didn't know what she wanted to hear. Merle was always the one who had a smile and all the right words. She just stood beside him, complementing him. He could carry the weight of the conversations, the social interactions, give her the bravery she needed to face large crowds of people.

She wished she'd thought to have brought a bottle of water. Her throat was dry; she couldn't swallow.

"I'm sorry for your loss."

Another hug, more perfume, more sorrow, more of her not knowing what to say, and then they walked off.

Lifting her chin, she looked at the large American flag flying between the two uplifted booms of the Mill Creek volunteer fire company. The breeze didn't seem like much, but it put ripples in the flag as it hung suspended high above everyone's heads.

It would make Merle's chest puff out to see it. He always had such pride in his country. And rightfully so. He'd been born with nothing, less than nothing, and he become a successful adult.

He'd had the house with a white picket fence, a wife, two small children, and a good job with great benefits.

A dangerous job.

That was the catch, she supposed. There was always a catch.

Two officers, their uniforms crisply pressed, their shoes sparkling in the sunlight, their hats tucked up underneath their arms, walked down past the fire trucks that hoisted the American flag.

The officers' jaws were set, their eyes determined. They weren't expecting to have fun. They were doing their duty. Mourning a friend. Determined to do their best, to pay their respects, to do what they would expect to do for them if life had gone differently.

"I'm sorry for your loss."

Another hug. More perfume. More uncomfortable silence while Annie tried to figure out what to say. She was sorry for her loss, too.

It wasn't just her loss.

Her eyes tracked across the well manicured grass to where her mom stood at the swingset, watching her boys play.

Justin, four, understood that daddy was never coming home.

Times of almost inconsolable crying followed by times of complete normalcy like he hadn't heard the daddy had been shot by someone who was attempting to rob a convenience store.

The convenience store was safe. The two employees who were on duty at the time were unharmed.

The armed thief was behind bars. For now.

And Merle...he lay in a box in the church behind her. After the pomp and circumstance of today, the lid would be closed forever, and he would be lowered into the hole that was now waiting at the cemetery just a few miles away.

She'd never been to a graveside service.

She wasn't worried about doing anything wrong. Not as much as she was worried about not being able to stop crying.

She didn't want that to be her last memory of her and her husband - her sobbing inconsolably at the edge of the hole in the ground where he would be laid to rest.

She swallowed again, listening to the snapping sound the flag made as the ripples caused by the light breeze shook out. Annie lifted her face to the air that brought the scent of flowers and spring and new birth.

She didn't want to forever associate that smell with sadness and death and devastation.

How could she not? This might not go down as the absolute worst day of her life, the day she found out about Merle would probably have that honor, but this would be a close second.

"I'm sorry for your loss." Another perfunctory hug, more perfume, stronger this time and it made her dry throat close as she had to swallow the heaving of her stomach.

She tried to smile, tried to look like everything was going to be okay, tried to pretend she wasn't fighting back tears.

Although, everyone would expect her to cry. No one expected her to stand here stoically. She was the only one who couldn't stand the idea of spending the entire day crying.

Crying might be cathartic for some people, but it only made her feel worse.

As though it were possible to feel worse than what she already felt.

A man who looked vaguely familiar strode toward her and she fought the urge to run away.

Merle had so many friends, both from his time in the Air Force, and his time as a volunteer firefighter, and from his job on the police force. She couldn't keep track of all of them. Couldn't keep the names straight. Couldn't remember who he knew from where. Not that anyone expected her to, she just liked to have that information organized neatly in her brain. But it wasn't.

Everyone had told her she was too young to get married. Too young to pledge her life to a man who was a decade older than she. But, she had fallen hard for Merle, and he had done the same for her. She thought they could overcome any obstacles life would throw in their path.

And they had. Until last week.

Death wasn't exactly an obstacle to overcome. It was a part of life that one had to walk through. And, when that death was one's husband, one had to work through it alone.

Not entirely alone. People wanted to help, she just didn't know how to let them. Didn't know what she needed. Didn't want to be touched or comforted or even to have company. It was all she could do to get her boys up in the morning and get them dressed and try to act and talk to them like life was still going on.

Thankfully her mother had flown in from her home in Sweet Water, North Dakota. Unfortunately, her mother was trying to talk her into going back out with her. She couldn't. She had the house to take care of, loose ends to figure out, and she already had enough changes in her life. She didn't want to uproot her boys and move across the country. Indiana was a long way from North Dakota.

The man was almost to her now, and no name came into her head. She might have only ever seen a picture of him. Once in a while Merle would talk about his buddies, show her pictures and tell her story.

It had always been obvious to her that the memories he had of his time in the Air Force were good. Of course, Merle loved everything he did; he loved serving as a volunteer firefighter, and had loved his job as a police officer, too.

He was in front of her now. The idea that he was from Merle's time in the Air Force tipped in her brain.

"I'm sorry for your loss." The man spoke, his voice holding authority as well as compassion. The kind of voice that will had confidence and determination like life was going to go the way he wanted to.

He was much older than she was, Merle's age, but she could disabuse him of the notion. She'd been disabused of it herself recently.

Life didn't go the way a person wanted it to, no matter how hard a person worked for it. God seemed to love pulling the rug out from underneath people so they could fall flat in their faces and wallow in their pain and misery.

"I'm sorry for it too," she said, not sure why those words came out. And now. They sounded bitter and more than a little angry.

The man blinked. He probably wasn't expecting an outburst like that. She presented a picture of youth and innocence, at least that's what she'd been told. She assumed that even though she felt like she lived a lifetime in the last week, she hadn't aged that much.

If the man were religious he might offer her a platitude about God knowing best.

If he wasn't, might agree with her that life did suck.

Or, he might not say anything, like so many people, and herself, who didn't know what to say.

"If you don't mind, I'll be around tomorrow. I owe Merle something, and I didn't want to give it to you today."

She lifted her chin, hoping that was good enough to let her know that she didn't care what he did. Come around, don't come around. At least he wasn't trying to tell her that God had everything in control. After all, who could believe in a God that will take two little boys' fathers away from them? Who would allow her world to be upended, after she'd chosen to go against the advice of the world, and marry the man she knew the Lord had for her.

He had for her, only to take him away.

Life wasn't fair, and it was really hard to believe that God was good right now.

She thought the man might hug her. Everyone else seemed like they wanted to, but he just looked at her, his eyes searching as though seeing under the surface expression of her face, down into her broken heart and broken spirit. Past the tears she wasn't allowing fall, and into the spot that felt empty and dark, like it would never live again.

"I know Merle had a lot of newer friends, good friends, but I just want you to know that if you need anything, anything at all, you don't have to worry about it, because we will help you."

It wasn't until he said that "we," that she realized there were several men standing around behind him.

Funny how she only saw him. She would have sworn he was the only one walking toward her.

Five. Her grief must have affected her vision. That, and the fact that she hadn't eaten for several days. She couldn't get food to slip past the lump in her throat.

"Thanks," she said softly. Happy to hear that the bitterness and anger that had been in her earlier words was not coloring those.

There was some murmuring from the other men around him, then the group strode off, the blonde man in the lead.

It wasn't hard to picture Merle walking with a group of men. Talking and laughing. Slapping each other's backs and smiling proudly at his wife and kids. Calling her over, tucking her under his arm introducing her.

She turned away, not wanting to see the reminder of everything that was wrong. Not wanting to wonder why it was her husband who had died. It was a terrible thought, she had to banish it from her head more than once. Because it kept coming back. Taunting her. She didn't want to be that kind of person. Didn't want to be the kind of person who doubted God the second something terrible happened to her, but how could she not?

She turned, knowing it was time. Time for her to go into the church, sit down at the front of it, beside the coffin, her boys on either side of her, and sit through something she never thought she would, the funeral of her husband.

Pick up your copy of *Just a Cowboy's Lifetime Love* by Jessie Gussman today!

# A Gift from Jessie

*View this code through your smart phone camera to be taken to a page where you can download a FREE ebook when you sign up to get updates from Jessie Gussman! Find out why people say, "Jessie's is the only newsletter I open and read" and "You make my day brighter.  Love, love, love reading your newsletters.  I don't know where you find time to write books. You are so busy living life. A true blessing."  and "I know from now on that I can't be drinking my morning coffee while reading your newsletter – I laughed so hard I sprayed it out all over the table!"*

*Claim your free book from Jessie!*

# Escape to more faith-filled romance series by Jessie Gussman!

***The Complete Sweet Water, North Dakota Reading Order:***

Series One: Sweet Water Ranch Western Cowboy Romance (11 book series)

Series Two: Coming Home to North Dakota (12 book series)

Series Three: Flyboys of Sweet Briar Ranch in North Dakota (13 book series)

Series Four: Sweet View Ranch Western Cowboy Romance (10 book series)

***Spinoffs and More! Additional Series You'll Love:***

Jessie's First Series: Sweet Haven Farm (4 book series)

Small-Town Romance: The Baxter Boys (5 book series)

Bad-Boy Sweet Romance: Richmond Rebels Sweet Romance (3 book series)

Sweet Water Spinoff: Cowboy Crossing (9 book series)

Holiday Romance: Cowboy Mountain Christmas (6 book series)

Small Town Romantic Comedy: Good Grief, Idaho (5 book series)

True Stories from Jessie's Farm: Stories from Jessie Gussman's Newsletter (3 book series)

Reader-Favorite! Sweet Beach Romance: Blueberry Beach (8 book series)

Cowboy Mountain Christmas Spinoff: A Heartland Cowboy Christmas (9 book series)

Blueberry Beach Spinoff: Strawberry Sands (10 book series)